Terminated
at the
Trailhead

NIGHTMARE
ARIZONA
PARANORMAL COZY MYSTERIES

BETH DOLGNER

Terminated at the Trailhead
Nightmare, Arizona Paranormal Cozy Mysteries, Book Nine
© 2025 Beth Dolgner

ISBN-13: 978-1-958587-29-4

Terminated at the Trailhead is a work of fiction. Names, characters, places, and incidents either are the products of the author's imagination or are used fictitiously. Any resemblance to actual persons, living or dead, businesses, companies, events, or locales is entirely coincidental.

Published by Redglare Press
Cover by Dark Mojo Designs
Print Formatting by The Madd Formatter

https://bethdolgner.com

CHAPTER ONE

I sucked in my breath and felt my fingernails digging into the skin of my palms. The day was cool, but sweat broke out on my forehead. "I can't believe you talked me into this, Justine!" I lamented.

My eyes were fixed on the scene in front of me, but I heard Justine's voice coming from behind. "Oh, come on, Olivia. You enjoyed flying with Gunnar, so why wouldn't you like this, too?"

"This is different!" My body tensed as the brown-and-white horse I was riding stepped over low rocks on the trail.

Laura, who was leading our excursion, turned in her saddle to glance at me. "Relax, Olivia. You have a death grip on the reins. Horses can tell when you're nervous."

I did my best to uncurl my fingers, but I knew Sweet Sugar wasn't going to fall for it. I hadn't liked horseback riding when I was a kid, and I didn't like it as a middle-aged woman.

"It's not your fault, pretty horse," I whispered to Sweet Sugar. "I like petting you and watching you perform in the stunt show."

In a louder voice, I explained to Justine, "When I flew with Gunnar, my life was in danger. I had no choice but to let him pick me up and fly away. Besides, if I had been too scared, I could have simply asked him to put me down."

"You weren't in danger," Laura pointed out. "You were running away from me."

"Yes, but we didn't know that at the time, because you were in your werewolf form."

"Fair point," Laura said.

"Also," Clara piped up in her high, childlike voice, "you can't ask Sweet Sugar to put you down, but you can ask him to stop. All you have to do is pull the reins." She was riding somewhere behind me, and she sounded like she was having a ball. I assumed fairies had a way with animals, because I knew she didn't ride horses often, but she had jumped on her black horse and started riding like it was something she did every day.

Zach, who was riding along the trail in front of me, threw a sly look over his shoulder. "At least our plan is working," he said. "We wanted to distract you from the fact your boyfriend isn't here, and I'd say we're succeeding. Admit it: you're too nervous to even think about how much you miss Damien."

Zach had a point, and I grudgingly said so. Damien Shackleford and I had been dating for a couple of months, and I had been missing him even more than expected during the past ten days that he'd been gone.

Damien had arrived in Nightmare, Arizona, about the same time as I had, returning to his hometown to help run his father's business, Nightmare Sanctuary Haunted House. But, at the same time, he was actively working alongside all of us to find his father, who had disappeared without a trace a year before.

We had finally gotten a lead that indicated Baxter had been taken by a faction of supernatural creatures—criminals, really—but we had hit another dead end. So, Damien had packed up and hit the road to visit some of the other

2

supernatural communities around the Southwest, hoping to learn anything that might help us find Baxter.

Months before either Damien or I had arrived in Nightmare, the other residents and employees of the Sanctuary had done the same thing, but this time, we had more details and were armed with better questions to ask.

Like, for instance, whether or not anyone had heard rumors about a captive phoenix, since that was what Baxter really was.

The trail turned left and began a sharp descent, and I grit my teeth as I leaned back in the saddle. "I should have gone with Damien," I muttered.

"Aww, do you miss your boyfriend?" Clara called. I couldn't see her or Justine, but I could hear the two of them snickering.

My friends and co-workers at the Sanctuary had been teasing me relentlessly about Damien, but I was past the point of feeling embarrassed about it. I was dating an incredibly handsome, kind, and supernaturally powerful man. Why would I blush about that?

"I do miss him," I said proudly. In fact, Damien had called me that morning, right before I headed to the Wild West Stunt Show to meet up with my friends for our adventure on horseback. Laura was the show's horse trainer, and she had thought it would be fun to exercise the horses and get all of us out on the trails at a nearby state park.

I had to admit it was a nice day for being out in nature. Some plants were already beginning to bloom, even though spring hadn't yet arrived in other, colder parts of the country.

I was admiring a bush with vibrant pink flowers when I sneezed. *Stupid allergies.*

I was trying to enjoy myself. Really.

The trail stopped going down, and I was relieved to be

on even ground again. We followed a curve to the right, and suddenly, the scrubby trees and low vegetation were interrupted by a black asphalt parking lot.

"We could have driven here?" I asked.

"Where's the fun in that?" Laura countered.

The trail widened, and Zach nudged his horse forward until he and Laura were riding side by side. He reached out and gave her arm an affectionate squeeze. The two of them had been dating for slightly longer than Damien and I had been, and seeing Zach's romantic side was almost—not quite, but almost—worth the nerve-racking time on a horse. He was normally a bit grouchy, and it was downright adorable to see how happy he was with Laura.

Zach and Laura both began waving in the direction of the parking lot, and I looked over to see Morgan, Madge, and Maida standing there, waving back. The three witches were clustered around a picnic table, and a couple of large pieces of paper were spread out in front of them, along with two bowls and a bundle of incense that smoked from its perch on a brass plate.

"Are they doing a spell?" I asked, more to myself than anyone else.

Clara appeared next to me as my horse stopped of its own accord, following the example of Zach's and Laura's horses ahead of it. "They're trying a locator spell," she answered. "Those are maps of Georgia, since that's where the Dire Market is."

The supernatural black market was a place for less-scrupulous supernatural creatures to buy, sell, and trade all manner of things, from items for working dark magic to pre-made curses. If our theory was correct that Baxter was in the hands of a faction called the Night Runners, who were some of the biggest traders on the Dire Market, then it was likely we would find him there.

I felt a hand on my knee, and I looked down to see

Justine, who had climbed off her horse already. "Come on, I'll help you get down."

My dismount wasn't the most graceful, but I was proud of myself for not falling over while trying to swing my leg up and over the saddle so I could climb off Sweet Sugar. I thought I detected a hint of relief in his eyes as I stepped away.

Justine, Zach, and Laura tied the horses' reins to a section of wooden fence between the trail and the parking lot while Clara and I headed for the witches.

"Good morning," Madge said, smiling at us. She was wearing a long fitted white dress paired with a light-knit shawl. Her golden curls spilled over the baby-blue yarn.

"Yes, a good morning for spell work," added Morgan. As usual, she was wearing a long black dress that looked two sizes too big for her withered frame. She pushed a strand of white hair out of her wrinkled face and lifted her eyes to the cloudless sky.

"And a good morning for putting fear aside." That third piece of advice—aimed at me, I was certain—came from Maida, the youngest of the witches. She looked like she was only about ten years old, though I knew she was likely much older. Even Madge, who didn't look a day over thirty, was probably decades older than me.

I touched a hand to my face self-consciously, wondering if people thought I was older than my forty-two years.

Madge seemed to sense my thoughts, because she laughed softly. "You look exactly as you should," she said. "Especially now that you have your feet firmly on the ground."

My laugh was much more boisterous than Madge's. "My discomfort on a horse is that obvious?"

The three witches nodded in unison.

By that time, the others had joined us, and Madge

motioned for all of us to gather around the picnic table. We stood in a circle around it, looking eagerly at the items spread out in front of us.

"This spell must be worked near rushing water from deep in the earth," Morgan said.

"And there happens to be a little spring-fed brook that crosses that trailhead over there," Madge added.

"But we can't find Baxter without a connection to him." Maida raised a hand, a shimmering red-and-orange phoenix feather held tightly in her fingers. We had obtained it through a somewhat-dubious tooth fairy named Orin, who was also involved with the Dire Market. To the best of our knowledge, the feather had come from Baxter.

Morgan began to chant softly while Madge and Maida each picked up one of the bowls. The one Madge held had a dark liquid in it, and she stirred it with an ornate silver spoon. Maida's bowl was filled with what looked like sawdust, and I instinctively leaned backward when it began to smoke.

Madge and Maida joined the chanting, and out of the corner of my eye, I could see other visitors to the state park staring in our direction. I couldn't blame them. It wasn't every day you went out for a hike and ran into witches doing a spell.

Morgan gestured to Maida, who sprinkled her still-smoking sawdust or pencil shavings or whatever it was across the maps spread on the picnic table. Once there was a fine layer of the stuff on top of the maps, Madge tipped her bowl and began to pour the thick liquid in a spiral shape.

I wasn't sure if the rest of us were supposed to remain silent during the spell, but I couldn't help the quiet "wow" that escaped my lips. The liquid began to move, mixing with the stuff Maida had sprinkled onto the maps to form a sort of putty-like substance. It stretched into a line, looking almost like a small snake that curled and slithered across the table.

The movement continued for a few moments, the magical snake moving slowly from one map to the next, then back to the first. Then, it slid to the edge of the table and slithered right off it onto the ground.

Morgan sighed wearily. "We did the spell correctly, but we have failed to locate Baxter."

Madge's beautiful face looked sad. "It's possible he is held somewhere that is warded against magic."

"But perhaps we can search for him a different way." Maida made a quiet sound, like she was deep in thought.

"We appreciate you trying," Justine said.

Morgan squared her shoulders, though it didn't do much to make her look any bigger. "Let us look at the bright side. It is a beautiful day, and we are here with friends. We brought a picnic lunch for everyone!"

I had to laugh at the black sedan Morgan moved toward. *No brooms for these witches,* I thought. The rest of us joined her to help set up our lunch, and soon, the maps of Georgia had been replaced with sandwiches, potato salad, coleslaw, and brownies. We didn't all fit around the picnic table, but Zach and Laura both said they were happy to stand, and Maida ate her sandwich while stalking crows who were sitting on a low branch nearby.

After we had eaten and packed up, we thanked the witches. I thought about asking for a ride back to town, but I stopped myself. I needed to put my fear aside, like Maida had said.

I climbed back onto Sweet Sugar even more awkwardly than I had gotten off of him, but soon, we were riding downhill on a different trail than the one we had been on before lunch. The parking lot was lost to view behind us, and we were beginning to climb up again when

Laura suddenly brought her horse to a halt. She leaped from the saddle and hurried forward.

It was clear from Laura's body language that something was wrong, so the rest of us quickly dismounted, too. Well, everyone but me. I was the last to join the huddle at one side of the trail.

There was a man sprawled on top of the dirt and weeds, and he was clearly dead.

CHAPTER TWO

We all stood silently for a few moments, staring at the body.

It was Clara who finally broke the silence. "Maybe he's just sleeping?" she squeaked.

"I'm pretty sure he's dead," Justine said.

Zach bent at the waist to get a closer look. "Oh, yeah, he's been dead for a while. And he's not just dead. This guy was murdered."

"How can you tell?" I asked, squinting at the body. I should have been grossed out, but I was so shocked by the scene I felt disconnected from it. It seemed unreal.

Zach pointed. "See those dark splotches on his shirt? He was stabbed, a lot."

Justine muttered a few words, including one I knew she would never say in polite company. "Olivia, I'm going to stop hanging out with you. I only see dead bodies when we're together."

"I told you riding horses was a bad idea," I intoned.

Clara held out her hand, her cell phone clutched in her fingers. "There's no reception out here."

"We'll take the horses back to the stunt show," Laura said, "and while we're riding, we'll call the police as soon as we get a signal." I was impressed by how calmly she was dealing with the situation. But, then, there had been a murder at that very stunt show she was referring to, so this wasn't her first go-round with death.

"Clara and I will stay here," Justine said. "Someone needs to keep an eye on the body."

Zach hitched up a shoulder in half a shrug. "Why? He's not going to get up and go anywhere."

Justine didn't bother to retort. She just rolled her eyes.

Soon, Justine, Clara, and the murdered man were on their own, and the rest of us were heading back in the direction we had come from. Zach had his phone in one hand, and I could tell he was looking at the screen more than the trail ahead, anxious to get a signal.

I quickly realized I should have stayed behind with Justine and Clara. Zach and Laura were each leading one of the riderless horses, but their pace was much quicker than I was comfortable with. With every little dip in the trail, I could imagine exactly where I would land when I lost my balance and fell off my trotting horse.

"Don't let me fall off, okay, Sweet Sugar?" I begged.

We passed the parking lot and kept going. After almost twenty minutes of riding, Zach shouted for us to stop. He held his phone to his ear, waited, then grumbled, "No, not yet. Keep going."

After another ten minutes, we repeated the same scene.

That morning, we had started our adventure by riding across barren fields that connected the stunt show to the network of trails at the state park. It wasn't until we were riding across those fields again that Zach called us to a halt for a third time.

The call went through, and I heard Zach's end of the conversation as he reported what we had found. Once he hung up, he called to Laura and me. "Let's get the horses squared away, then we'll drive back to get Justine and Clara. The police should be there by then."

It took a while to get the saddles and bridles taken off

the horses, but eventually, they were secured inside the corral next to the stunt show's barn. I felt a lot more comfortable behind the wheel of my old clunker of a car than I did at the reins of a horse, and I drove as fast as I dared back toward the state park.

I found the parking lot easily enough, and I pulled in next to the two police cars and one ambulance that had already arrived.

Zach and Laura had been faster than me on horse-back, but that was nothing compared to their speed on foot. As werewolves, the two of them moved a lot faster than a plain-old human like me. I finally gave up trying to match their pace, and I slowed to a fast walk. *Maybe,* I thought, *I'll catch my breath before I reach the crime scene.*

By the time I arrived, the area had already been cordoned off with yellow crime scene tape, which looked incongruous among the scrubby trees and sun-bleached vegetation of the high desert.

Luis Reyes was standing in front of Clara and Justine, his pen flying across the small notebook he always carried. As I got within hearing range, he looked up at the two women. "And that's all you can tell me?"

Clara shrugged. "We just spotted him on the side of the trail. There's really nothing more to say."

"Of course. It's just that, usually, when someone from the Sanctuary finds a body, one of you has a connection to the murder."

"We don't know this guy," Justine said. Her voice sounded strained, and I knew it was because she didn't like Reyes's implications. The two of them had been on a couple of dates recently, and while Justine wouldn't tell us much, it was clear she had enjoyed getting to know Reyes better. He was trying to do his job at the moment, but his connection to Justine was making it very awkward.

"Officer Reyes," I began. "Er, Luis." He and I had

agreed to be on a first-name basis since we ran into each other so often, but in situations like our current one, it was hard not to revert to something more formal.

"Of course you're here, Ms. Kendrick," Reyes said with resignation. "When Justine said the others would be arriving shortly, I knew you would be one of those others. I can't get through a single investigation without you being a part of it."

I gave a little shrug. "It's not my fault. Any idea who this guy is?"

Reyes pressed his mouth into a thin line. "Since there doesn't seem to be any connection between the victim and the Sanctuary, I'd like to keep it that way. I'm not sharing any details, because this murder has nothing to do with any of you."

I had to admit that was fair, but I was also too curious to give up so easily. "Is it normal for people to get murdered on trails around here?"

Reyes gave me an exasperated look. "We don't even know that he was murdered."

"But—" I cut off at a sharp look from Justine. Instead, I sighed heavily. "You're right. It's best to let the police do their work."

Reyes put his pen and notebook back into the breast pocket of his uniform, then ran a hand through his dark hair. The hard look in his reddish-brown eyes softened as he gazed at Justine. "I'm sorry you had to go through this today. I know it wasn't the fun day of riding you were hoping for."

Justine gave Reyes a sad smile. "Like you said, though, at least it has nothing to do with any of us."

"We need to get our investigation underway, but I'll call you later?"

Justine nodded before turning away. It was clearly our cue to head out so the police could search the area for evidence, and before long, all five of us were crammed into my car.

On our drive back to the stunt show, where Justine had parked her car that morning, I glanced at her in the rear-view mirror. "Zach told us that man was murdered," I pointed out. "Why didn't you want me to say so to Reyes? Er, Luis."

"Because I took a closer look at the body while Clara and I waited for all of you to get back," Justine said. "Zach was right about the guy being stabbed to death."

"Then the police must have noticed the telltale signs, too," I noted.

"I'm sure they did. And they'll be trying to solve a stabbing case with a body that they think has been lying there for a while, judging by the state of decomposition."

"I feel a big 'but' coming," Zach prompted.

Justine sighed. "But that man was already dead when he was murdered. He was a ghoul."

CHAPTER THREE

I was trying so hard to absorb Justine's pronouncement that I forgot to keep my foot on the gas pedal. The car slowed, and it wasn't until the car behind me honked that I realized what I was doing.

"Did you say a ghoul?" I asked as I sped up.

I was confused, but Laura and Zach chorused, "Oh, of course!"

"I should have realized," Zach said. "That wasn't a body that's simply been lying in one place for a while. The matted hair, the filthy clothes… That was a dead body that was on the move before it was killed."

"Can someone please explain?" I asked. Since arriving in Nightmare more than six months before and learning supernatural creatures really did exist, I thought I had gotten pretty good at rolling with the surprises. If fairies like Clara existed, then a tooth fairy like the one I'd met not long ago wasn't too much of a stretch. I had seen Zach transform into a werewolf once, so I wasn't overly shocked when the Sanctuary's resident banshee foresaw a death.

But a ghoul? A dead person who had been murdered?

"You all realize how ridiculous this sounds, right?" I asked. "I thought ghouls were creepy dead people who stalked old cemeteries, kind of like zombies. And, just like zombies, I thought ghouls weren't real. Just legends that make for great horror films."

"Sorry to burst your bubble, Olivia," Justine said, "but ghouls are real."

"And your description of them isn't far off the mark," Zach added. "Ghouls are reanimated corpses, and it's usually done through magic. A ghost takes over a dead body—sometimes its own body, but not always."

"Why?" I asked. If I ever came back as a ghost, I doubted I would want to inhabit a rotting corpse.

"To get revenge, or maybe take care of some unfinished business," Laura answered. "You know, typical ghost stuff. Having a body helps the ghost accomplish more."

"However, the magician who raises a ghoul—" Clara began.

"The resurrectionist," Zach interrupted.

"Yes, the resurrectionist often does his work for a price: the ghoul has to perform some task before it's allowed to go off and do, well, whatever it wants to do. Usually, though, the corpse gets too gross before the task is finished, so the ghoul never gets to take care of its own business."

I frowned. "Sounds like resurrectionists have quite a racket going. A disgusting, gross, smelly racket."

Zach, who was in the passenger seat, nodded. "If any of us dies with a score to settle, I do not recommend coming back as a ghoul."

"You mean I should settle my scores now, while I'm living?" Justine asked. "Because you still owe me twenty bucks from our last poker night, so you'd better pay up before I croak."

I was so absorbed in the discussion I nearly missed the turn that led to the stunt show, and I braked hard so I wouldn't miss the street. "Sorry. I'm too distracted by this whole concept. You're saying the murder victim probably hadn't been lying there as long as it looked like."

"Exactly," Laura said. "I rode that trail three days ago, and there was no dead man. Someone killed him a while back in some other location, and he wound up becoming a ghoul. That ghoul was out on the trail at some point in the past three days, and someone killed it."

"Which means the police are going to be so confused," I noted. "No one called in a dead body until today, even though it appears the guy was killed days, or even weeks ago."

"They're going to have a tough time of it, that's for sure," Justine agreed. "And it's entirely possible the guy wasn't even killed for the first time here in Nightmare. The murder might have happened somewhere else. I hate to say it, but Luis may not get to close this case, because he doesn't know about the supernatural world. I can't tell him the truth."

"Which means Olivia is going to want to dive in to solve the murder, and she's going to drag all of us along for the ride," Zach said. He threw me a look that I'm sure was supposed to appear accusatory, but I could see his eager smile.

"Let's assume the ghoul was out there on the trail because he was performing some kind of task for this resurrectionist," I said. "What could that task possibly be? He was on a hiking and horseback riding trail in a state park."

My question was met with silence, until Clara eventually said, "The ghoul's body might have bitten the dust, but the ghost that was inhabiting the body could still be hanging around. We should ask Vivian to look for it."

"She'll be in the middle of packing," Justine pointed out. "But, yes, if she has time, it could be really helpful."

Vivian was the Sanctuary's resident psychic. Like the rest of us, she was anxious to find Baxter and bring him home. She and her husband, Amos, had volunteered to drive to the East Coast to look for signs of Baxter on the Dire Market. They were scheduled to leave for Georgia soon, and they had been hoping the witches could give them a clear starting point for their search.

Since the witches hadn't been able to successfully pinpoint a location for Baxter, I figured Viv and Amos were going to have a long search ahead of them. I was hopeful, but I wasn't holding my breath.

We had reached the stunt show by that time, and I pulled into a parking space next to Justine's car. Clara was already pulling out her phone to call Vivian as we climbed out of the car, and Laura made a beeline for the barn so she could check on the horses.

That left Justine, Zach, and me.

"What now?" Justine asked.

Zach shrugged. "Laura will have the midday stunt show soon, so she's got to get to work. I guess I'll go back to the Sanctuary and warn the others that we stumbled on a ghoul today."

"Why warn them?" I asked. "It's dead, so it can't hurt anyone."

"But that ghoul was out there on the trail for a reason, which means whomever put it there is likely up to no good." Justine shuddered. "Never trust anyone who uses dead bodies to get something done."

"I have a question," I began.

Zach and Justine both laughed. "Sometimes," Justine said, "I forget how new you are to all of this."

"To be fair," Zach said, "I've only heard about ghouls. Today is the first time I've ever seen one."

Justine nodded. "Me, too."

"I'm glad we could all have this magical experience together," I said sarcastically. "Here's what I don't get. If a ghoul is already dead, then how do you kill it?"

"Simple," Zach said. "You feed it."

"Feed it what?"

"Food. Any kind of regular food is all it takes. Did you notice what was on the ground next to the ghoul? A porterhouse steak. A bite had been taken out of it."

I shook my head. "Nightmare has had some strange murders since I got to town, but this has to be the weirdest. Somebody murdered a dead guy with a porterhouse."

Clara had just rejoined us, and she smiled as she slid her phone into her pocket. "Vivian says she can meet us in an hour, so why don't we hang out here for a bit? The stunt show's concession stand has ice cream, and I'm starving. That picnic lunch feels like ages ago."

I was about to point out that ice cream wasn't the most nutritious choice for a lunch—well, second lunch—but since Clara was a fairy, she had a serious sweet tooth. Plus, after our adventure, maybe we all deserved a little ice cream as comfort.

Before long, my friends and I were leaning against the corral fence with ice cream cones in our hands. People were beginning to arrive for the first stunt show of the day, and we were content to watch them go past as we waited until it was time to meet Vivian at the state park.

My cone was half-eaten when Sweet Sugar snuck up behind me and thrust his head over the top of the corral fence. "Sorry, buddy, but I don't think ice cream is good for horses," I told him apologetically. I did give his nose a good rub, though. Sweet Sugar and I got along a lot better when we both had our feet firmly on the ground.

We waved goodbye to Laura when it was time for us to leave. She was saddling the horse ridden by the star of the stunt show, and she wished us luck as she adjusted the strap on the saddle.

Vivian and Amos were waiting for us when we arrived in the parking lot at the trailhead. Amos had a worn wooden box in one of his large hands.

"I see you brought help," I said to Amos, gesturing at the box. "Good thinking."

"They're just waiting for some privacy before they come out," Amos answered. He nodded his head toward a spot behind me, and I turned to see a family climbing out of a car.

"I think it's going to be an even longer wait than that," Justine said. "The police cars are still here."

Vivian waved dismissively. "I don't need to go all the way to the crime scene. I just need to be in the general vicinity." She reached up and adjusted the green scarf tied around her head. "If there's any ghost around, I'll be able to feel it."

Amos looked down at his wife and smiled proudly. I always liked seeing the two of them together, because he was big and burly, while she was petite, with a fashion sense that seemed to come right out of the nineteen fifties. They were such a contrast to each other, but it somehow worked, and I thought Amos and Vivian were the cutest supernatural couple in Nightmare.

Well, after Damien and me, of course.

Once the parking lot had emptied, I felt a cold wave of air against my left arm.

"Miss Olivia," drawled a voice. "Justine, Zach. I'm pleased we can help bring another criminal to justice."

"Hi, McCrory," I said. I could barely make out his black duster and cowboy hat. It was a lot harder to see the ghosts when we were out in the sunshine, but I could just make out McCrory's bushy black mustache. "Where's Tanner?"

"Up here."

I looked over to see Tanner seated cross-legged on top of Amos's car. "Why are you up there?"

"The high ground is always the better spot," he answered. His head slowly swiveled from left to right, and his eyes were narrowed above the red bandana he always wore. "Just keeping an eye out."

It had been well over a century since Butch Tanner and Connor McCrory had killed each other in a legendary shootout on High Noon Boulevard, but the outlaw and the sheriff hadn't changed a lot, it seemed. Their ghosts were tethered to the six-shooters they had used in the shootout, and those were safely nestled inside the wooden box Amos was carrying.

We set off down a trail that, according to the map posted at one side of the parking lot, ran parallel to the trail where we had discovered the ghoul. That way, Vivian and the ghosts could get close to the crime scene, but we wouldn't be spotted by the police.

Not that it would matter if we were, since we weren't doing anything wrong, but I didn't think they were ready for two ghosts and a psychic to be on their investigation team.

We had been walking for about five minutes when Vivian stopped abruptly. She bent forward and clutched the sides of her head.

At the same time, McCrory moved slightly in front of me, his arms held out like he was trying to shield me.

"We have to leave," Tanner said, his voice tight. "Right now."

"What's wrong?" I asked. Nothing looked amiss to me, and there was no one else on the trail. "Is the ghost of the ghoul angry?"

"They're all angry!" Vivian said. She was still holding her head in her hands, but she began to back away. "This place is crawling with ghouls!"

CHAPTER FOUR

Amos put an arm around Vivian's shoulders, then steered her in the direction of the parking lot as we turned and hurried toward it. None of us said a word as we walked, but I could tell from Justine's and Zach's body stances that they were on high alert, just like me.

It had been bad enough seeing a dead ghoul, but I definitely didn't want to run into a living one.

By the time we reached the parking lot, Vivian had dropped her hands. "We're far enough away now. I'm okay."

"How do you know you were sensing ghouls rather than normal ghosts?" I asked.

Vivian tilted her head thoughtfully. "A ghost that's inhabiting a body feels dark. Putrid, almost."

I nodded. "Like the body itself."

"Exactly!" Vivian closed her eyes and raised her hands. "I could feel six of them, all ahead of us, but spread out."

"The question, then," Zach said, "is who put them there, and why?"

"And should we track all of them down and feed them ice cream cones?" I added.

Tanner and McCrory were all for that suggestion. Once the ghosts had been separated from the bodies, they explained, it would be a lot more comfortable for them to try communicating with their fellow specters. They whole-heartedly agreed with Vivian's assessment of how it felt to be in the presence of a ghoul.

"I think," Justine said slowly, "we shouldn't do anything right now."

When Tanner started to protest, Justine raised a hand to stop him. "As far as we know, the ghouls haven't hurt anyone. If we leave them where they are, we can keep an eye on them, and that might help us learn what's going on."

"But can't we communicate with their ghosts?" I asked. I was kind of liking my ice cream plan.

"There's no guarantee the ghosts will stick around," Vivian said. "They might cross over as soon as they're no longer possessing a body. Justine is right. Waiting and watching is the best thing we can do."

"The Sanctuary is closed tonight," Zach said, "which means we can send out a group to keep watch as soon as it's dark."

"I'll come hang out in the dark," I volunteered.

"And I'm sure we'll have help," Justine said, nodding. "Theo complains his life isn't as dangerous as it was when he was a pirate, so I bet he'd love to face down some ghouls."

"And some of us used to suspect Malcolm was some kind of ghoul, so this seems like a perfect job for him," Zach added.

"Did people really think that about Malcolm?" I asked, wrinkling my nose. He was one of the best-dressed people at the Sanctuary, and he certainly didn't look like he was dead.

On second thought, he kind of did, with his high cheekbones and sunken eyes. Malcolm gave off more of a skeleton vibe than a rotting corpse vibe, I decided.

We thanked Vivian, Amos, and the ghosts for their

help, then split up. Justine and I had both driven to the trailhead, so she took Zach and Clara back to the Sanctuary, where they all lived. I headed home to Cowboy's Corral Motor Lodge.

I dashed into my little efficiency apartment to take a quick shower and put on fresh clothes. I figured I must smell like horses and fear at that point. Since it was such a nice day out, I opened the window next to the kitchenette and enjoyed the fresh breeze and the sunshine that brightened the look of my rust-orange shag carpet.

Once I was clean, I walked up to the front office of the motel. My apartment was at the rear of one of the two wings that ran back from the street. Between those wings, near the street, was a two-story cinder-block building that housed the motel's office. The drives into and out of the parking lot were on either side of it.

There was something comforting about the tinkle of the bell above the glass door as I walked into the office. Like my apartment, the office also had shag carpet, but it was light brown, and the whole place screamed retro-kitsch, right down to the Formica check-in counter.

Mama's hair was the first thing I saw when I walked in. It was gray and voluminous, like a fluffy raincloud, and since she was sitting at the desk behind the counter, it was all I could spot of the woman who ran Cowboy's Corral with her husband.

Mama popped into view as she stood up, a wide smile on her face. "Hello, welcome to— Oh." Mama's smile disappeared. "Oh, Olivia, tell me what happened."

I gave a little laugh as I looked down at my jeans and fuchsia knit top. "How can you tell?"

Mama made a *tsk* noise. "It's not how you look. It's how you feel."

"I should have realized you'd pick up on it."

Mama had started showing signs of being a psychic

when she was a preteen, but she had purposely tamped down her abilities, choosing to live as normal of a life as possible.

Except, it was impossible for her to completely rid herself of the talent, so she was unusually perceptive. I had learned that if Mama ever got bad vibes from someone, then that was a person to avoid.

I began to give Mama the rundown of what had happened that morning, and when I got to the part about the murder victim having been dead already, she sucked in her breath.

"A ghoul!" she said, her bright-blue eyes wide. She was still standing behind the Formica counter, and she braced her hands on the edge of it.

"Even *you* have heard of them?" I asked. "I thought the concept sounded a bit far-fetched."

Mama released her grip on the countertop and laughed. "But sirens, vampires, and werewolves aren't?"

"Well, but, at least those supernatural creatures are alive," I said lamely.

If I'm just now learning about ghouls, what else is out there in the supernatural world?

"Tanner and McCrory are dead, too," Mama pointed out. "But I do understand what you mean. The walking dead are something we associate with horror movies, not real life. Anyway, I'm glad to hear the one you found on the trail was already dead for good."

I pursed my lips. "Then you're not going to like the rest of my story." I told Mama about our return to the state park and Vivian's report that there were another half-dozen ghouls wandering the area.

"I don't like it. Not at all," Mama said when I had finished. "Where there are ghouls, there's trouble."

I smiled. "That sounds like a homily my grandmother

would have said to me, if she had ever heard about ghouls."

"Speaking of grandmothers," Mama said, her face lighting up as she leaned to look past me. "I've been told I'm the best one in the world, because I agreed to keep Lucy after school every day this week."

I didn't need to turn around to know Mama's grand-daughter was walking through the door right then. The bell clanged a lot louder when a ten-year-old was pushing the door open, and I heard three rapid footfalls before scrawny arms wrapped around my waist.

"Grandma! Miss Olivia!" Lucy buried her head against my side, her mass of brown curls bouncing, then released me and dashed to Mama, so she could repeat the process.

"How was the bus ride, dear?" Mama asked.

"Fine," Lucy said, the faintest hint of a pout on her lips. "But not as cool as when you pick me up from school."

Mama drove a red vintage Mustang. If I had been Lucy, I would have pouted about having to ride the school bus instead, too.

"I'll make it up to you," Mama said. "Go upstairs, and you'll find your favorite snack in the fridge."

"Ooh, yes!" Lucy pumped a fist and pelted up the stairs. There was an efficiency apartment up there, similar to mine, but Mama and Benny used it as a sort of retreat from the front desk rather than a living space.

I breathed out a sigh of relief after Lucy had disap-peared. "I'm glad I got to fill you in before she showed up."

Mama nodded. "She's too young to be thinking about such dark subjects."

The bell sounded again, and I turned to see a man stalking through the door. He was tall and lanky, and his unkempt brown hair hung down past his shoulders. His weathered face had a scowl on it, but I didn't get the impression it was directed at me or at Mama.

This, I thought, *is the kind of guy who looks angry all the time.*

He was also the kind of guy who, for lack of a better term, gave me the creeps. Bad vibes, as Mama would say.

Hey, maybe I'm becoming a little bit psychic, like Mama.

I stopped celebrating my burgeoning ability to read people so I could listen to what he was saying to Mama.

The man had stepped past me, and he leaned his elbows on the countertop. "Do you have security cameras here?" he asked.

"Yes," Mama said. She was eyeing the man in a way that let me know she felt the same way about him as I did.

"Can you please tell me where they're located?"

"Mr., ah, Culver, I believe it is? Are you worried Cowboy's Corral is dangerous?"

"Not your motel itself, no." The man hesitated, threw a glance at me, then leaned closer to Mama. "I just want reassurance that unsavory characters aren't sneaking in here."

Mama's mouth opened, then closed. Finally, she said, "Nightmare is a quiet town, Mr. Culver. And while we do have our fair share of unsavory characters, as you call them, they aren't skulking around my motel."

"The location of the cameras?" Culver prompted.

Mama jerked her head toward the left. "There's one trained at the entrance to the parking lot." Her head then went right. "And one at the exit. Both drives are covered."

"What about the entrance from the alley out back?"

"It's just a walkway, not a driveway. What's a criminal going to do, steal your belongings, then walk all the way home with them?"

The man said something under his breath, and I caught the words "vehicle" and "waiting." While he was

28

right that someone could park in the alley behind the motel and get onto the property on foot, I didn't think it was a likely scenario.

"I don't have any cameras trained on the rooms themselves, because guests deserve their privacy," Mama said pointedly.

That, at least, was something Culver didn't argue with. He muttered a thank you, then turned and left.

Once the door had closed behind him, I said, "That was strange."

"*He's* strange," Mama said without hesitation. "Both him and the guy he arrived with."

"Are they causing problems?" I wasn't sure what I could do if they were, of course.

"No, they're both laying low. It's just the feeling I get from them."

I nodded. "Even I can sense the creepy."

"There are a lot of rumors going around Nightmare at the moment. Those unsavory characters Culver mentioned? The rumors say shady people have been arriving in Nightmare the past few days. No one knows who they are, or why they're here."

"And now, we've got ghouls descending on Nightmare, too." I frowned.

"I don't know what's going on," Mama said, "but it's not good."

CHAPTER FIVE

When I arrived in Nightmare, I had been absolutely broke. Mama had taken pity on me, offering me the efficiency apartment in exchange for doing marketing work for the motel. These days, I had enough money coming in from my work at Nightmare Sanctuary Haunted House that I could afford to move elsewhere, but our arrangement worked so well I didn't want to leave.

Plus, Mama had started to feel like family, and I liked knowing she was just steps from my apartment all day, every day.

I had some marketing work to take care of that afternoon, so I set up a makeshift office in the lobby, settling into a sagging old chair and sipping on the always-scalded coffee Mama kept hot on a nearby table. I told Mama I was working there because I didn't want to be cooped up by myself in my apartment, but she called me out on the lie instantly.

"You're keeping an eye on me," she said. She winked at me. "I don't need protection, but I appreciate it, anyway."

It was nice to have a quiet, relatively normal few hours after my very bizarre morning. A number of people came in to check in for a stay that night, but Culver never reappeared. I got a lot of tasks accomplished, and by the time I shut the heavy old laptop Mama had loaned me for the job, I felt a sense of satisfaction.

When I told Mama I needed to go get ready for some ghoul watching, she raised a finger and said, "You be careful. Make sure Damien is with you, because I know he'll keep you safe."

I patted a back pocket of my jeans, where my cell phone was stashed. "He's in Surprise," I said. He had called during the course of the afternoon, and we had exchanged a dozen text messages since then. After talking with the supernatural community in the small town of Surprise outside Phoenix, Damien was planning to head east to the Superstition Mountains, where there was rumored to be a vampire enclave.

"Oh, I keep forgetting he's gone." Mama sighed. Damien was her nephew, and she would also be happy when he returned to town. "Will Malcolm be going tonight?"

"I believe so."

"Then you stick close to him. I'd put my money on a wendigo over a ghoul any day."

I promised I would do that, then left. It was still daylight out, and I would have loved to have walked to the Sanctuary to enjoy the nice evening, but I drove instead. If Mama and that character Culver were right about unsavory characters descending on Nightmare, then I needed to be cautious.

Nightmare Sanctuary Haunted House was a little over a mile away from Cowboy's Corral, down a two-lane road that passed along a grove of pecan trees. Giving someone directions to the Sanctuary was easy: keep driving until you see the old gallows, then turn right. That narrow little lane led directly to the front of the former hospital building.

Since the Sanctuary was closed on Tuesday nights, none of the exterior lights were on as I drove toward it.

Normally, the lights gave the weathered stone facade a spooky-but-inviting glow. Tonight, though, the building looked dark in the growing twilight. Only the bright light coming from some of the windows reminded me that, inside, everything was warm and friendly.

I wasn't surprised to find the double front doors locked, and I knocked loudly in the hope someone would hear me and come let me in. As I waited, I heard a low grumble behind me.

Do ghouls make that kind of noise? I thought wildly as I slowly turned around.

To my relief, it wasn't a ghoul standing there but a chupacabra. I squatted down and held out a hand. "Felipe! Come here, boy."

Felipe trotted over and rubbed his leathery gray snout against my hand.

"Did you go out the doggy door out back?" I cooed. "Did you want to go out and play before Mori wakes up?"

"He can't answer you," Zach called from behind me. He had responded to my knock, but I hadn't heard the door open.

"I know chupacabras can't talk," I said as I stood.

"You're not going to start talking to me like that when I'm in my wolf form, are you?"

"Why wait?" I asked. I stepped forward and ruffled Zach's long red hair. "Who's a good accountant? You are!"

Zach wiggled out of arm's reach as I laughed and breezed past, Felipe on my heels. Zach was, hands down, the grumpiest person at the Sanctuary. He was a lot more personable when he was with Laura.

For that matter, he was a lot more personable during the three days of the full moon, when he was a wolf.

"What's the plan?" I asked as Zach shut and locked the door behind me.

"The vampires aren't awake yet, but we assume they

want to help with our ghoul stakeout, too. The rest of the gang is in the dining room."

"Is Laura going to join us tonight?" I asked as we walked through the wide, high-ceilinged entryway and headed down a hallway to our right, which led to some of the staff-only areas of the Sanctuary.

"Probably not. She's got to get through tonight's stunt show, then she plans to stay in the barn for the rest of the night. She's worried a ghoul might come sniffing around."

I stopped walking and gave Zach a horrified look. "Ghouls eat horses?"

"No, they don't need to eat, remember? They only eat when someone deliberately feeds them." Despite his grumpiness, Zach reached out and put a comforting hand on my shoulder. "The horses might get spooked if they saw a ghoul. That's it."

I let out a breath I didn't realize I had been holding. "Sorry," I said. "This whole walking dead thing is new to me, and it's making me a little jumpy."

Add in the creepy guest at Cowboy's Corral, and I might be jumping at shadows tonight.

When Zach and I walked into the dining room, the first thing I saw was Malcolm, who was pacing back and forth in front of the high windows that looked out over the wild area behind the Sanctuary. It was nearly dark outside, and I knew Mori and Theo would be waking up soon.

The second thing I saw in the dining room was our resident gargoyle, Gunnar. The fact his presence wasn't the first thing to catch my eye showed just how far I had come in acclimating to the supernatural world. In addition to his hulking size and sinewy wings, Gunnar was also notable for his skin, which looked like gray stone that had a light covering of greenish moss on it.

"You're joining us tonight?" I asked happily.

Gunnar grinned at me, his sharp teeth on full display.

"I'll be providing aerial support. If I spot anything from the air, I'll radio Zach, since there's no cell phone signal out there at the park." He waved a walkie-talkie, which looked tiny gripped in his clawed fingers.

I peered at Gunnar. "You can radio someone while you're flying?"

"Sure. I just have to be careful not to drop it!"

I didn't ask Gunnar where he stashed his radio when he wasn't using it. Gunnar didn't see the point in wearing clothes, probably because he looked like a statue.

"Our crew on the ground then is Zach, Malcolm, and me?" I asked.

"I'm only staying for a while," Zach said. "I'm going to join Laura to keep her company."

"But I'm in!" I heard a voice say behind me. A pair of strong hands landed on my shoulders, and Theo leaned his head close to mine, his mouth uncomfortably close to my neck. "Just as soon as I grab a quick dinner."

I squirmed my way out of Theo's grasp. "Don't dine on me, please," I said. "I need my strength for tonight."

"Besides, I don't think Damien would take it well if he hears you've been chewing on his girlfriend." It was Mori, who glided past us.

"I do not chew on people," Theo said, shaking his head. His shoulder-length brown hair moved in time with the motion.

Of the two vampires at the Sanctuary, only Mori still had her fangs. Theo's had been filed down by a vampire hunter, back during his pirate days. He had to use a small knife to draw blood, instead, but since vampires could mesmerize people, he never got any complaints.

"I need dinner, too," Mori said. She batted her golden eyes and smoothed her black hair, which was pulled up in a high coiffure befitting a woman who had been a countess a couple centuries before. "It won't take me long to snag a tourist. I'll bring Felipe along with me. He'll enjoy the outing."

Theo and Mori both said they would meet us in the parking lot of the state park. With that settled, the two of them left after saying they were heading toward High Noon Boulevard, where tourists would still be roaming around. The vampires preferred feeding from people passing through, rather than locals who might get suspicious.

No sooner had the vampires left than Justine and Clara joined us, but Justine skipped right over a hello and led with, "We're not heading out on the trails with you."

Clara nodded. "It's likely the ghouls are only there at the state park, but just in case, we're keeping a watch both here at home and at my family's bar." Under the Undertaker's was a bar exclusively for supernatural creatures, and while Clara's aunt was a tough one to get past at the door, I could understand why Clara wanted to help keep an extra eye out.

Zach was anxious to get started, but Malcolm insisted on ducking into the kitchen first to get some snacks.

"For us, or for any ghouls we might encounter?" I asked.

"Both," Malcolm answered with a shrug.

Half an hour later, I was pulling into the parking lot of the state park again. It wasn't until that moment that I realized how much I did not want to be walking down the trails, in the dark, when there were ghouls on the loose.

I was the last one to climb out of the car, and as I did, I saw the breeze lift the hem of Malcolm's long black coat. He had worn his usual black top hat, too, even though our task was hardly an occasion for formal headwear. His pale skin seemed to glow in the light of the half moon that shone down on us.

To anyone else, Malcolm would have looked terrifying.

I found it comforting. Mama had been right to suggest I stick close to him for safety.

There was a soft thud behind me, and I yelped as I whirled around. I should have known better, though, because it was just Gunnar, who had landed right next to my car. "First Felipe tries to give me a heart attack, and now you," I muttered, but it was too low for Gunnar to hear.

"Theo and Mori should be here shortly," he reported.

Sure enough, the vampires joined us just ten minutes later, though to me, it felt like an hour. I was on high alert, and with every minute that ticked by, I was getting more skittish.

As soon as our group was complete, we set off down the trail. I was the only one who required a flashlight, and luckily, I had one in my glove box. I kept it trained on the ground right in front of me as we walked, afraid of taking a bad step in the darkness.

"He can sniff out ghouls," Mori said as we walked. She nodded toward Felipe, who was on a leash so he wouldn't take off into the underbrush. "At least, I assume he can."

I had just stopped jumping at every little sound in the night when Felipe began to strain against his leash. He growled, and Malcom leaned forward, his dark eyes searching the area Felipe was trying to move toward. "I smell it, too."

"Smell what?" I asked in a timid voice.

"Death."

Mori and Theo agreed, and I shuddered. If the ghouls were close enough to smell, then why couldn't we see one of them?

I was about to point out that my presence was perhaps unnecessary, since I couldn't smell anything out of place, when Mori said, "Olivia, you should try conjuring a ghoul to come close to us."

"You know my conjuring only works when I'm focusing on something I really, really want, right?" I tried to make it sound lighthearted, but I knew it came off as scared.

"We really want to know what's going on," Theo pointed out.

I took in a deep breath, closed my eyes, and thought, *I want a ghoul to come close so we can get some answers. I want to learn more about why there are ghouls here.*

What I really want right now is to be curled up with Damien on his couch.

"Stop it, Liv," I said out loud.

"Stop what?" Malcolm asked.

"Wishing for the wrong thing." I shook my head, like I could fling my thoughts about Damien right out, then went back to focusing on conjuring a ghoul.

It didn't take long.

There was the distinct sound of footsteps walking toward us from somewhere up ahead.

CHAPTER SIX

My eyes snapped open, but there was nothing to see. The curve in the trail ahead meant we would just have to be patient.

We all remained silent, and Malcom carefully moved slightly in front of me, shielding me from the approaching ghoul. At the same time, I half-turned my body, ready to turn tail and run. It wasn't the bravest of plans, but it seemed like a good one.

The footsteps grew louder, and suddenly, a form appeared on the trail ahead. A man was walking toward us.

A man who was absolutely alive.

The man stopped abruptly and stared at us. Then, with a tight smile and a little nod, he continued on his way. We all parted to let him pass, staring after him with open mouths.

"Not a ghoul," Theo said under his breath once the man's footsteps had faded away.

"There weren't any other cars in the parking lot," I pointed out.

"It's awfully strange that someone is out walking the trails at night," Theo continued.

"Without a flashlight," I added.

Malcolm gave a low laugh. "Just imagine what he thought when he saw us. Talk about awfully strange."

Zach and Theo both voted for following the man, but the rest of us cautioned against it. For all we knew, he was just out for a hike, and we didn't want to make the guy uncomfortable.

"I guess my conjuring kind of worked," I said. "I made someone appear, but it was someone who was alive. I knew as soon as I saw his pristine skin that he wasn't a dead guy."

"Pristine?" Mori said, looking at me judgmentally. "That man has never seen a bottle of moisturizer."

"I think Olivia's point is that the guy wasn't rotten," Malcolm said.

"If you were all smelling death, then how is it that the person we saw is alive?" I asked. "And does that hiker have any idea what's lurking out here?"

"Probably not." Zach yawned and stretched. "I'm going to need so much coffee to stay awake with Laura tonight. Anyway, I can still get a whiff of death, so there's at least one ghoul in the area. Olivia, I think you should try your conjuring again."

I reluctantly agreed. I was a lot more powerful when Damien was with me because his abilities—we weren't quite sure yet what those were, exactly—seemed to amplify mine, and vice versa. Still, it was worth a shot.

For the second time, I closed my eyes and thought about how much I wanted to learn why there were ghouls roaming around the park. In my mind, I even saw what looked like a zombie from a low-budget horror movie, but he was wearing hiking boots and cargo shorts.

I even heard a low sound, almost like a moan.

When someone near me sucked in their breath, I realized the sound hadn't come from my imagination. I kept my eyes squeezed shut for a few moments longer, not wanting to see what was making that sound. Then I realized I would much rather know what I was facing.

Malcolm and Zach were both bent forward slightly, their shoulders rounded and their feet planted like runners preparing to take off. Their predatory natures had kicked into high gear.

The low sound was coming from somewhere ahead, and Felipe was scrabbling against the hard-packed dirt, trying to move closer.

Slowly, everyone else began to walk forward, not making a sound.

"Come on," Zach whispered to me. I was the only person not moving.

We rounded the curve in the trail, then stopped where another trail crossed the one we were on. I couldn't hear anything, but Felipe was trying to turn left, down the other trail. Mori leaned forward, listening, then gave a firm nod, and we took off in that direction.

The ghoul was standing in the middle of the trail, just a short distance away. I could only see its silhouette in the pale light of the moon, but I could sure smell it.

"Olivia, shine your flashlight on it," Malcolm said softly.

"Ew, no, I don't want to see it!"

"Then don't look."

I raised my flashlight to illuminate the creature, but it wasn't as horrible of a sight as I had anticipated. In fact, I was less disgusted by the thing shambling toward us than I had been by the murder victim we had found out on the trail earlier that day.

"Oh, it's not so bad," I said.

Theo snickered. "You don't like looking at me when I have my zombie makeup on, but you're okay with this guy?"

"The ghoul is far away," I noted. "You like to get up

close and personal when you're looking particularly gruesome."

The ghoul was not, in fact, wearing hiking boots and cargo shorts, but what I had envisioned hadn't been too far off the mark. It was dressed in what looked like khaki pants and a dirty, ripped T-shirt for a baseball team. Its hair was sticking out in every direction, and it looked like it was dark-blond underneath all the grunge.

Felipe had been staring silently at the ghoul, but he suddenly made a sound that was somewhere between a bark and a howl. Even though I knew Felipe was a friendly chupacabra, the sound sent a shiver down my spine.

As Felipe's cry echoed, the ghoul finally seemed to notice us. Its pale, unfocused eyes looked at each of us, then it slowly turned and began to shuffle in the opposite direction.

And here I was preparing to sprint back to the car if we were attacked. I made a mental note that ghouls were remarkably slow, and I felt a bit of my fear drain away.

We followed the ghoul for about fifteen minutes. Of course, at ghoul speed, that wasn't all that far along the trail. Up ahead, there was yet another trail crossing ours, and I was wondering which way the ghoul would choose, when Felipe veered right, into the underbrush.

"Olivia, shine your flashlight this way," Mori requested. "I want to know if Felipe has caught sight of a possible snack for himself, or something worse."

My flashlight didn't show anything in the tight cluster of low trees, and Mori called Felipe three times before he finally relented and returned to the trail.

A few feet later, Malcolm stopped, but he was facing left. He sniffed the air, then his body tensed up. "We need to leave, right now," he said in an even voice. He turned toward the rest of us and held his arms out, the edges of his cape gripped in his fingers. It was like a screen that blocked the ghoul from our view, but Malcolm seemed to be doing it as a way of hurrying us along. He came right at us, and our choices were to either turn and hustle toward the parking lot or get caught up in Malcolm's cape.

I, of course, was the slow one, so Malcolm was right on my heels.

"What is it?" I asked him, panting as I went as fast as I could.

"We'll talk about it at the Sanctuary."

Ahead of me, I heard Zach speaking in a low voice, but I was too busy trying to navigate the trail—which wasn't easy in the dark, even with the flashlight—to pay attention to what he was saying.

Suddenly, a dark form filled the empty space in front of me, and I shrieked. I abruptly stopped running, and Malcom plowed into me from behind.

"So dramatic," Gunnar said. He had landed just inches from me, and I knew Zach must have called him on the radio. "Come on, you know how this works." Without waiting for acknowledgment, Gunnar deftly spun me around, wrapped his arms around my waist, and lifted me into the air.

Gunnar grumbled when he smacked into a branch of an ironwood tree that dangled over the trail, but he didn't seem hurt, and we rose higher. "To the parking lot, please," I called over my shoulder.

This is so much better than riding a horse.

In no time at all, Gunnar was smoothly landing right next to the driver's side door of my car. I had just gotten the car unlocked when the others came running up. Since Theo and Mori were with us now, that meant it would be a squeeze on the drive back, but Mori shouted, "I'll catch a ride with Gunnar!"

I got the car started as Theo, Zach, Malcolm, and Felipe piled in. They all, including Felipe, yelped with fear as I careened out of the parking lot.

"I envy Mori," Zach said. "I should have thought to fly with Gunnar."

Felipe made a rumbling noise, and Malcolm added from the back seat, "Can chupacabras get car sick?"

Hearing such a bizarre question made me laugh, despite the urgency Malcolm had made me feel, and I eased off on the gas pedal. After all, ghouls couldn't move fast, and even though I was still learning about them, I was pretty sure they couldn't drive. We were out of whatever danger Malcolm had perceived.

Nevertheless, he refused to explain our sudden departure until we were back at the Sanctuary, saying it would be easiest to tell it once, after we met back up with Mori and Gunnar.

As it turned out, Malcolm had a much bigger audience than that. Gunnar could fly faster than I could drive, and he and Mori had gathered as many people as they could before we arrived at the Sanctuary. I was surprised when I walked into the dining room to find nearly the entire staff assembled there.

Clara gave me a wide-eyed look as I sank down onto a bench at one of the long wooden tables lined up in the room. "Did anyone get hurt?" she asked.

I shook my head, then gestured toward Malcolm. He was stepping up to the podium that sat on a low platform at one end of the room. "I'm as curious as you are to know what happened, and I was there," I told Clara.

Before he addressed all of us, Malcolm leaned forward and spoke to someone sitting at the table directly in front of him. I saw Maida, the youngest witch, pop up and run out of the room, her tall black boots tapping across the stone floor.

"I'm glad to see all of you here," Malcolm began, "because I think everyone should know what's going on here in our town." He then gave a brief account of the murdered ghoul, and Vivian's report that there were at least six more ghouls wandering around the state park.

By the time Malcolm had reached the point in his narrative about a group of us going to the park that evening, Maida had returned with a piece of paper in her hands. She hurried to the podium and handed it to Malcolm.

"We were here," Malcolm said, holding up the paper and pointing at a spot. I could see it was a state park map Maida had brought him, and he began to note other places with a bony finger. "We weren't *following* the ghoul tonight. It was *leading* us right into a trap. Felipe smelled one on our right, and I caught the scent of another to our left. They were slowly surrounding us."

"Why are they there?" Justine piped up.

"It's hard to say," Malcolm said. "We don't know who resurrected them, or why they were left out there in the wilderness."

The discussion continued for a while, but none of us had the answers. Eventually, Malcolm conceded that continuing to speculate was pointless, and our impromptu meeting wrapped up. It was too dangerous to return to the trails, so I said goodnight to everyone and got ready to go home. After such a wild day, I was ready for bed and some ghoul-free time.

Malcolm walked me to my car, even though we knew we were well out of danger, and I headed home with a lot to think about. I went to bed shortly after I got back to my apartment, but I didn't sleep a lot. My brain was still trying to sort through everything I had experienced in less than twenty-four hours.

I had set my alarm for ten o'clock the next morning,

but it was my phone ringing that woke me up. As soon as I saw the call was from Luis Reyes, I was wide awake. "Reyes?" I answered. "I mean, Luis?"

"We went back to the state park early this morning to search some more," he said grimly. "It's a good thing, too, because we found another body. This one is fresh."

CHAPTER SEVEN

"Another body?" I repeated. "How close was it to the first one?"

Did someone take out another ghoul?

"It was about a quarter of a mile away, sitting right at the trailhead near the parking lot," Reyes answered. I couldn't see him through the phone, but I could picture him shaking his head. "I know you and Justine, and the rest of your group, said you told us everything yesterday, but I thought it was worth calling all of you, just in case you could remember more details that might help us understand what's going on."

"We actually went back to the trails last night," I confessed.

Reyes sighed. "Looking for clues on your own again?"

"No." I hesitated. I couldn't tell Reyes we had been a scouting party on the lookout for ghouls, but I realized it seemed odd that we had gone out for a nighttime hike. That thought made me gasp. "Oh! We saw someone, out there on the same trail where we found the man yesterday."

"At night?"

"Yeah. It was a man in dark pants and combat boots, and he was wearing a black sweater. His face was really tanned and weathered, and he had dark-brown hair. Is that the same person you found this morning?"

"No, that's not our victim, but he certainly might be a suspect. After all, who in the world goes for a hike after dark? Well, aside from you and your friends."

"I wish I could tell you more, but we didn't talk to him. I think he was as startled by us as we were by him. I do remember being surprised to run across anyone, because the only car in the parking lot was mine. I'm not sure where the man came from, or how he got to the trails."

"There are some campsites around the state park and a couple of smaller parking lots off other roads," Reyes said. "The lack of a vehicle isn't strange in and of itself. What's strange is that the hiker, as well as you Sanctuary folks, might have been out there around the time this second murder happened."

"Second murder?" I asked. "You're confirming the guy we found yesterday was killed?"

Reyes chuckled. "You already knew that, because there's no way you and your friends missed the stab wounds. Other than the hiker, did you notice anything else last night? Noises, lights?"

"No, nothing," I said. I hated having to lie to Reyes, but again, I couldn't casually drop the word "ghoul" in conversation with someone who didn't know about the supernatural world. The closest Reyes got to any of that was his affinity for visiting a psychic on a regular basis.

Reyes sighed. "It's too bad. Like I said, the murder might have occurred around the same time you were out there, since this body was fresh."

"That's the second time you've used the word *fresh*," I pointed out.

"Because the first body was already decaying signifi-cantly when it was found. It had obviously been there for a while, so how no one had seen it yet is beyond me. Those

48

trails are popular at this time of year, when the weather is so nice."

If only you knew, I thought. Reyes was right about the decay, but so wrong about how long the ghoul had been sprawled on the side of the trail.

"It's not always easy to determine a time of death when you've got nature in the equation," Reyes continued. "Indoor murder investigations tend to be a lot easier."

"How was this second victim killed?"

Reyes was silent for a moment, and I assumed he was having an inner debate about how much to tell me. Finally, he said, "This victim was also stabbed. Olivia, you and your friends need to be careful. I think it's possible there's a serial killer in Nightmare. No more nighttime hikes, okay?"

I was sitting up in bed, looking at my kitchenette and the small table with two chairs. Suddenly, the whole scene seemed to tilt a little bit. My mind had gone back to the trap the ghoul had been trying to lead us into the night before. If Malcolm hadn't realized what was happening, would Reyes have found our bodies that morning?

No, I told myself firmly. First, only Zach and I would die if someone stabbed us, and that only applied to Zach if the knife was silver. Second, I had no idea how ghouls killed, but I was pretty sure it wasn't by stabbing. They could barely walk, and I doubted a ghoul had the dexterity to wield a knife.

Even if they could, they would be moving so slowly their intended victim would have plenty of time to fight back or run.

So, then, who had killed the man found on the trail that morning? Was our mysterious nighttime hiker responsible? Had we nearly caught him in the act?

"Olivia?" Reyes prompted.

I shook my head. "Sorry. I was just thinking through

49

what you said about a possible serial killer. Do you think it's someone local?"

"Who knows? Neither victim had a wallet, which means no ID, but this latest victim did have a keychain for the University of North Carolina. It's likely he was..." Reyes trailed off, then laughed self-consciously. "Sometimes, I forget you're not an official part of the Nightmare Police Department, since you always wind up in the middle of our investigations. I need to keep quiet until we find out who the victim is and notify his loved ones."

"Of course," I said quickly. "I understand."

"I'd better go. I need to call Justine and fill her in, too."

"You should tell her over breakfast," I suggested.

Reyes sounded disappointed as he answered, "I wish I could, but I'm on the clock. I'm afraid these two murder investigations are going to cut into my free time for the foreseeable future."

I wished Reyes luck—both with the investigations and with Justine—before hanging up. Then I sat there, phone in hand, for a long while as I digested everything Reyes had told me. The second victim gave me a whole new perspective on our outing the night before. We had been in danger both from the ghouls and from whatever living person had stabbed Mr. North Carolina.

There was no point in lingering on such dark thoughts, so I got up, showered, and got ready for my day. I had just poured my first cup of coffee when there was a quiet knock on the door.

It was just a few minutes after ten o'clock, so it was unlikely to be one of my friends from the Sanctuary, since they all preferred a nocturnal lifestyle. It was more likely to be Mama or her granddaughter, Lucy, so I opened the door with a smile on my face.

My smile got a whole lot wider when I saw Damien standing there. He grinned at me, his green eyes glowing softly. The waves of his dark-blond hair caught the morning sunlight, and he looked more handsome than ever.

He's only been gone two weeks, and I already forgot how good-looking he is.

"Damien!" I nearly shouted as I threw my arms around him. He gave me a tight squeeze, then leaned back slightly so he could give me a kiss.

"Surprise," he said. "And by surprise, I mean I'm here when you didn't expect it. I don't mean Surprise, the town I visited yesterday. After I talked to the vampire enclave in the Superstition Mountains last night, I decided I was ready to come home. I wasn't learning anything helpful about my father, and I missed you. A lot."

"Did you drive all night?" I asked.

"I got home around three o'clock this morning. I knew you'd be asleep, so I went home and did the same." Damien still had a tight grip around me, and I leaned into him. I had to crane my head up to look him in the eye, and he bent down and planted a little peck on my nose. "Would you like breakfast?"

I sighed. "Yes, but first, I need to fill you in on the latest."

Damien's expression instantly changed to one of worry. "What's wrong?"

"We are all fine," I said firmly, and I knew Damien realized I meant not just all of us at the Sanctuary, but Mama and her family, too. I had already told Damien about the dead ghoul we found on the trail, so as I took his hand and led him inside, I began with, "A group of us went back to the state park last night, and we managed to find a ghoul. Unlike the one we found yesterday, though, this one was still alive. Well, he's a ghoul, so he's dead already, but you know what I mean."

"That's not good," Damien said tightly.

"And right before you arrived here, I got a phone call from Officer Reyes about a second dead body the police discovered this morning. Unlike our ghoul, this victim was alive when he was murdered."

Damien dropped my hand and made a beeline for my coffee maker. He silently got a cup out of the cabinet, filled it, then refilled mine. Only once we were seated at the table did he wave a hand toward me. "Tell me everything."

I did. I even told Damien about the motel guest who had come into the office the morning before, asking strange questions about the security camera setup at Cowboy's Corral.

When I was done, Damien reached across the table and took my hand. "I don't like knowing you were in danger last night, but I'm happy you're safe now. Though I'm unsettled by this report that shady people are popping up in Nightmare. I don't think it's a coincidence they're arriving at the same time we're discovering ghouls in the area. Something big is going on, and I have to wonder if it has to do with my father."

"What makes you think that?"

Damien's gaze fixed on something to my right, but it was unfocused. Slowly, he said, "I don't know. It just feels like this all has to be related somehow. It's like"—Damien put the hand that wasn't holding mine over his chest—"a feeling? A sense?"

I smiled. "Your mother's psychic ability has been passed on to you, and you're starting to open up to it."

"Maybe." Damien's pensive face lit up as he returned his focus to me. "And, right now, my psychic senses are telling me that bacon and eggs on sourdough toast is exactly what I need."

"I'm thinking hash browns and an omelet." We had both finished our coffee, so I put our cups into the sink, and we headed out into a very pleasant morning. It was cool enough that I needed a light sweater for the walk to The Lusty Lunch Counter, but I knew it would be short-sleeves weather by the time we finished up.

During our walk, Damien filled me in on his visit with the vampire enclave in the Superstition Mountains. They had been wary, he said, but willing to help. Unfortunately, they hadn't heard any rumors about Baxter, the Night Runners, or strange activity in the area.

"None of the other communities around the Southwest have been able to help, though they were all friendly enough," Damien said as we walked up to the front door of the diner. The Lusty Lunch Counter was in Nightmare's oldest area, and the building looked every bit of its nearly one hundred and fifty years of age. The clapboard siding had once been painted white, but the paint had peeled away, leaving bare wood that had a gray, sun-bleached tone to it. One look at the two-story building, and it was clear it had been a part of Nightmare's Wild West history in the eighteen hundreds.

Inside, though, the place was a diner with a shining stainless steel counter fronted by stools and rows of booths with overstuffed red bench seats. Walking inside The Lusty Lunch Counter, whose name was in honor of the building's seedy past as a brothel, was like traveling back to the nineteen fifties.

Since it was nearing eleven o'clock, the breakfast crowd had cleared out, but the lunch crowd hadn't arrived yet. Damien and I slid onto stools at the counter as my regular server, Ella, bopped over to say hello and hand us menus.

As I pulled my menu toward me, I saw Jeff, the owner of The Lusty, walk out the door that led to the kitchen and his office. A man with a shaved head and intense hazel eyes was following him.

"Oh, Olivia, Damien," Jeff said. He spread his hands on the counter and leaned toward us. "I heard about the murders at the state park. You two know anything about that?"

Jeff had retired from his life as a hunter of supernatural creatures, and I wondered if he knew a ghoul had been one of the victims. Before I could ask, the man trailing after him leaned over the counter, as well. Jeff's stance was friendly, but the stranger's was threatening.

"You're from that haunted house," he said. From his tone, it was clear he knew the Sanctuary was populated with the same kind of creatures Jeff used to hunt down.

"And you," Damien answered, "are a hunter."

CHAPTER EIGHT

The man's face was unreadable as he stared at Damien. Beside him, Jeff stiffened.

Eventually, one side of the man's mouth turned up in a small smile. If he was trying to look even more sinister, then he was succeeding. "I'm just a friend of Jeff's," he said.

"This is Robert Pace," Jeff said, quietly enough that no one else in the diner would overhear. "He isn't here to cause any trouble. Robert needed to lay low for a while, and I told him he could stay with me. But he knows anyone from the Sanctuary is off limits."

"I'm sure that's going to make everyone feel safe," I said. I couldn't hide my sarcasm. Even though I had teamed up with a couple of hunters a while back to solve a murder that had happened right there in the diner, I wasn't comfortable feeling like the only thing between a hunter and my friends' safety was Jeff's request.

And, I realized, not just my friends' safety but mine, too. Back when I had teamed up with the two hunters, I had still been in denial that I was a conjuror. Now that I knew what I was, I realized I might wind up on a hunter's hit list, too.

Scary.

Damien was keeping his composure better than me,

because he sounded much more polite as he said, "We appreciate you giving us our space and safety. We're not bad people."

"So Jeff says." Robert glanced at his friend, then made a little noise of disappointment. "And I trust his judgment."

"Well," Jeff said in a falsely bright tone, "that was awkward, but I'm glad it's over with. We'll see you two later."

"Mama says shady people are showing up in Nightmare," I said in an undertone once Jeff and Robert had walked out the front door of the diner, "but it never occurred to me some of those people might be hunters."

"Like I said, something is going on, and I'm pretty sure it somehow involves my father." Damien sighed. "Right now, though, there's nothing we can do, so let's order, shall we?"

As we ate and chatted, I tried to keep myself in the present moment. Damien was back, and we were enjoying a nice breakfast together. I could shove thoughts about ghouls and hunters out of my mind for a while.

I wasn't entirely successful, but I did a pretty good job of enjoying breakfast.

After we wrapped up, we walked out of The Lusty and turned left, planning to take a different route back to Cowboy's Corral than the one we had taken to get to the diner. That took us right past the office for Emmett Kline, Nightmare's real estate king. He was just walking out the door of his office as we passed.

"Hi, you two!" Emmett called. He was immaculately dressed, as usual, and his tan suit looked more expensive than anything in my meager wardrobe.

"Hello, Emmett," I said happily. It had been a while since I had seen him, and even though he oozed salesman vibes, I still liked the guy. "Where are you off to?"

"Oh, I've got to meet a couple who wants to look at a house on the south end of town. Speaking of couples, I understand you two are dating now. You let me know when you're ready to look at some houses yourself."

Damien and I both burst out laughing. "We've only been dating a couple of months," I told Emmett.

Emmett was undaunted, though. "Your father, Damien, had strange taste in housing." That was an understatement, since Baxter had purchased an old mine and turned it into a home. Damien had been living there since his return to Nightmare. "Maybe you two would prefer to buy a patch of land and build something to suit your own tastes. It's always nice to get exactly the home you want, and I've got just the piece of land. It's up off Route 31, and the highest piece of the property gives you a great view out over the state park. Just imagine drinking your morning coffee on a big deck overlooking that serene setting."

"Sounds lovely," I said, suppressing a smile.

"You two let me know if you'd like to see it," Emmett said, smiling broadly. "In the meantime, I'm off to sell a house!"

Emmett bustled off, leaving Damien and me snickering.

"Just imagine," Damien said, "drinking our morning coffee while searching for ghouls wandering the wilderness."

"So relaxing," I agreed. "Sounds like a great way to start the day."

Our conversation with Emmett had been a bit ridiculous, but it was exactly what we needed to lighten the mood. As we continued our walk, I wasn't thinking about ghouls, hunters, or murder victims. Instead, I was enjoying the sunshine and Damien's company.

It wasn't until we were approaching the stairs that led

up to my second-floor apartment that all those things came crashing back into my thoughts.

There was a beat-up red sedan parked in the lot of Cowboy's Corral that had a North Carolina license plate. "North Carolina," I said quietly. "Reyes mentioned the murder victim—the real one, not the ghoul—had a North Carolina keychain. I wonder if he was staying here."

"We should tell Mama," Damien said. "You mentioned there was no ID on the body, but she'll have his name on file, and you can bet Mama remembers what the owner of this car looks like."

"She sure does, because he's not easy to forget." I pointed. "I'm pretty sure this car doesn't belong to the dead guy, but to the creepy guy."

Culver, the guest who had wanted to know about the motel's security cameras, was walking across the parking lot, and he was heading straight for the car I had spotted.

I moved to go talk to him, but Damien caught my arm. "He could be a hunter, too," he warned me.

"I doubt he knows I'm a conjuror," I said. "But I'll be careful."

"I'll be right behind you."

"Mr. Culver?" I called as I walked toward the man.

He paused and looked at me, then at Damien. "Yeah?"

"I couldn't help but notice your car is registered in North Carolina."

"So?" Culver's expression shifted from cautious to suspicious.

"Did you come to Nightmare with someone else?"

Culver crossed his arms. "You're nosy."

I shrugged. "So I've been told. Where is your friend?"

For a moment, I thought Culver was going to ignore me because he took a few steps closer to his car. I was surprised, then, when he answered, "We had a bit of a falling out yesterday. I told him to go find his own place to stay."

A bit of a falling out? Or a bit of murder? Maybe Culver had killed the guy in the course of their disagreement.

Because, way out here in Arizona, in the little town of Nightmare, there couldn't be that many people from North Carolina running around. I was almost certain the murder victim had been Culver's companion.

I considered asking Culver point-blank if he was a killer, but that seemed both unwise and impolite. Still, I needed to find some way of getting more details.

Before I could come up with a solution, I heard the squeal of tires and looked up to see a van hurtling toward us. Culver and I were both standing in the middle of the parking lot, and the front of the van was getting awfully big in my field of vision.

I'm not ready to die, I thought wildly.

Suddenly, my feet lifted off the ground, and my body sailed backward. I was flying through the air.

CHAPTER NINE

This is not at all like flying with Gunnar, I thought, just before I landed on the asphalt. I lay there for a moment, too stunned to move, as I listened to the van's tires screeching again.

Suddenly, Damien was crouched down next to me. "Are you okay?" he asked, his fingers gingerly pressing against my hands and arms to check for injuries.

"I think so." I wiggled my fingers and toes. "Nothing is broken, at least."

I sat up slowly and realized I was in the middle of an empty parking space, at least ten feet away from where I had been standing. Culver, I noticed, was huddled between two cars. He had jumped backward as the van approached.

I, on the other hand, had been lifted right off the ground.

"We just did that," I said.

There was no need to explain what I meant to Damien. He sounded proud as he answered, "We did."

What I had wanted most in those seconds before being run over was to not die, and Damien's psychic power had ripped me right out of harm's way. The two of us were becoming more powerful together, and it had just saved my life.

I kissed Damien's cheek before he took my hand and helped me up. I would probably have a few bruises on my backside from that landing, but I was otherwise fine. I brushed my hands over myself to get the dirt off, and when I looked up again, I realized Culver was staring at us.

"Uh-oh," I said under my breath. "Do you think he noticed?"

"Act casual," Damien advised.

That was pretty hard to do when my veins were full of adrenaline, but I knew what he meant. "Are you hurt?" I called to Culver.

He gave himself a little shake. "No. I knew a few folks were unhappy with me, but I didn't think they were that mad."

"Who was that driving the van?"

Culver shook his head. "I don't know. I got a look at the driver as he passed, but I didn't recognize him."

I had seen just enough of the driver to know it hadn't been the nighttime hiker, because the guy in the van had looked much older than him, right down to his lank gray hair.

"It wasn't your friend that you got in a fight with?" I asked.

"No."

I saw movement to my left, but instead of a speeding van coming toward me, it was Mama. I had never seen her move so fast. "What just happened?" She looked at me with a concerned expression, then glared at Culver. "I saw a van hightailing it out of the parking lot."

Since none of us had any apparent injuries, Mama's face relaxed. "Oh, hi, Damien. I'm so glad you're back in town."

"Hey, Mama," Damien said, reaching out to squeeze her shoulder. "And to answer your question, it appears the van driver was trying to run down this guy."

Mama's eyes narrowed. "Mr. Culver, what sort of trouble have you gotten yourself into?"

"Like I told these two, I knew I had some folks after me, but I don't know who that man was, or why he was trying to flatten me."

Mama shook her head. "It's not good to have so many people after you that you don't even know who might have just tried to mow you down. No wonder you were asking me about the security cameras here."

Culver had been looking at Mama defiantly, but he had the grace to say, "I'm sorry if I've put you or anyone else in danger. I'd better go."

As Culver moved toward his car again, I blurted, "Your friend went to the University of North Carolina, didn't he?"

Culver hesitated. "I think so. Do you know him? Why are you asking so many questions?"

I sighed. "I'm so sorry, Mr. Culver, but I got a phone call from the police this morning. They found someone with a University of North Carolina keychain out at the state park."

"Dead," Culver said. He wasn't asking. Maybe it was something in my voice or expression, but he knew.

"Murdered. I'm so sorry," I said again.

"Is that why you asked me about him? Because you suspected he was the person the police found?"

I nodded. "I saw the North Carolina license plate, and I thought maybe it had been the victim's car. Then I saw you heading for it."

Culver's face shifted, and his expression became impassive. I had no idea if he was mad, upset, or wholly unsurprised by the news. "Why would the police call you to share this information?"

It wasn't the question I had been expecting, and I fumbled my words until I finally said, "My friends and I were in the area of the state park last night, and the police hoped we might have seen something that would help them with this murder case."

Culver's eyebrows drew down. "You think I killed Vincent, don't you?"

"We have no idea who might have killed him," Damien said firmly.

Culver gave a curt nod. "I have to go," he said again. Without another word, he got into his car.

"I'll call Reyes and tell him we might have news about the victim," Mama said as we watched Culver back out and leave. "I heard there was another body found at the park this morning, but I never suspected it was someone who was staying here."

"We'll come with you to the office, and you can put Reyes on speaker," I said. "We need to tell him someone almost killed Culver and me both."

Damien took my hand and looked at me proudly. "On the plus side, your near-death experience was a great opportunity to use our combined powers."

"Oh, that makes me feel so much better," I said, winking at Damien.

Mama gave us a questioning look, and I explained how my desire to not die had worked with Damien's abilities to send me soaring through the air to safety.

"Good work, you two," Mama said when I finished. "However, let's hope Culver didn't notice the supernatural rescue."

"Luckily, he didn't ask me how I managed to fly, so I think we got away with it."

In just a few minutes, Damien and I were leaning across the Formica countertop in the front office while Mama sat behind it, dialing the police department on the phone. When Reyes came on the line, I gave him a quick rundown of my encounter with Culver and the intended hit on him. Then, we informed him that we'd identified the victim as Culver's companion, Vincent.

"Ms. Kendrick," Reyes began, then he sighed. I knew he was frustrated with me when he reverted to calling me Ms. Kendrick rather than Olivia.

"I know, I interfered in your investigation."

"I'm glad you have so quickly identified our latest victim," he said, "but, yes, you should have called me with your suspicion about the connection between the car from North Carolina and the victim. What if his friend is the killer? You just tipped him off that we're investigating the murder."

I shrugged, even though Reyes couldn't see me. "Mama had already heard the news this morning," I countered. "Word was already going around, so Culver would have known before long, anyway."

Reyes seemed to realize arguing the point was futile, since there was no denying there were few secrets in Nightmare thanks to the way gossip spread through the town like wildfire. Instead, he changed the subject. "You described the van, but not the driver. Did you get a look?"

"Older man, gray hair," I said immediately. "His hair was a bit messy, like he was really overdue for a trim."

"Anything else?"

"No. I was too busy trying not to die to notice details."

Reyes sighed again, but this time, he sounded less frustrated and more concerned. "I don't like that there was an attempt on a guest's life right there in the motel parking lot. And I especially don't like that he was willing to hit you, too."

"I don't like it, either," Damien grumbled.

"Damien, is there anything you can do to step up security at Nightmare Sanctuary?" Reyes asked. "If the van driver saw Olivia with Culver, then he might assume they know each other or are working together somehow. I don't want her or anyone else who works at the Sanctuary to be in danger."

I smiled. Reyes was talking about keeping me safe, but I figured it was Justine's safety he was really concerned with.

"We'll take extra precautions," Damien promised.

Once the call ended, Mama looked at Damien and me with an eyebrow raised. "So, what now?"

Damien and I stared at each other. We had no idea.

"I'm not sure what to do next," I said. "We've got a murdered ghoul, a murdered man, and at least three suspects."

"Three?" Mama asked. "Whom do you suspect outside of Culver and the van man?"

"The trail man." I told Mama about the man we had encountered on the trail Tuesday night, and she agreed it seemed strange for anyone to be out hiking in the dark.

"Four," Damien said suddenly. "We have four suspects, because I wouldn't rule out Jeff's friend Robert. We just found out there are ghouls in the area, and suddenly, a hunter shows up, too? There's likely a connection."

"Despite Robert and Jeff both denying it," I said.

I was trying to act like I was fine after the incident in the parking lot, but the truth was, I was shaken. It was bad enough someone had tried to run down Culver, but Reyes had made a good point that the driver had been willing to make me collateral damage. We were dealing with someone violent, and none of us knew who he was or where he might pop up next.

I made a mental note not to stand anywhere near Culver, if I ran into him again.

Damien seemed reluctant to leave me on my own, and he didn't head to his office at the Sanctuary until Mama promised she would keep an eye on me. I could sit in a lobby chair with my laptop, as usual, and work.

I jumped every time someone came through the door or a loud car roared by on the road, but I did manage to get a few things done.

When the bell above the door sounded shortly after three o'clock in the afternoon, I jumped again, but I relaxed as soon as I saw it was Damien. He had an odd look on his face, like he was surprised or confused.

"What are you puzzling over?" I asked as I put my laptop aside and rose to give him a quick kiss.

"No one at the Sanctuary knew I was back in Nightmare until I walked in there earlier," he said. "They seemed so happy to see me."

"Of course they were happy," I said. It was my turn to look confused.

Damien spread his hands. "It's just... When I came back to Nightmare last year to take over in my father's absence, I was so resentful, and everyone there seemed to feel resentful toward me."

"You were kind of a jerk," I reminded him.

"I know. I guess I'm just surprised at how much things have changed. The people at the Sanctuary have become my friends. They care about me. I knew that already, but today was a nice reminder."

"We all care about you, honey," Mama said. "Both your Sanctuary family and your blood family."

There was a rumble outside the office, and I looked up to see a beat-up tow truck coming to a stop. It was Nick Dalton, Mama's son. He rolled down his window and waved at us, then mouthed, "Gotta go!"

Even as he was letting us know he was in a hurry, his daughter came bounding around the front of the truck and into the office. Nick had picked up Lucy from school and was delivering her into Mama's care for the afternoon.

"Speaking of family," Damien said. "Hi, there, Lucy."

"You're back!" Lucy screeched. She threw her arms

around Damien. "We missed you a lot, but Miss Olivia missed you the most."

As Nick drove off, Lucy let go of Damien and said seriously, "I heard about the murder at the state park. How can I help?"

"What do you mean?" Mama asked.

"Someone here," Lucy said, looking directly at me, "likes to solve murders. So, I thought I would offer my psychic services. I've been dreaming about a woman who has the same name as me. She's teaching me how to talk to ghosts!"

CHAPTER TEN

"Tell us about this woman in your dreams," I said breathlessly.

"Lucille is really pretty," Lucy said. "She has kind of big hair, like Grandma, but hers isn't gray; it's brown. And she said that I'm going to be very good at talking to ghosts, but I have to practice my skills."

Mama had come around the counter to greet Lucy, and she stepped back to lean against it. Her face was so pale I instantly worried she was going to pass out.

"Mama?" I asked. I took a step toward her, but she waved me off.

"I'm okay." She sniffed and blinked back tears. "This is good news. It's nice to know Lucille is looking after Lucy."

Lucy tilted her head. "You know her?"

Damien had been silent since Lucy's pronouncement, and his voice was thick when he reached down and took Lucy's hand. "Lucille is my mom."

"And my sister," Mama answered. "Remember we told you that your great-aunt could talk to ghosts, too?"

"Oh," Lucy said. The emotion of the moment was lost on her, but I knew it meant a lot to Damien and Mama that Lucille was making her presence known, even if it was only in Lucy's dreams. Lucille had been such a powerful psychic that she had been able to shed her body, voluntarily becoming a ghost or an incorporeal presence, or whatever it was she had become. At any rate, she no longer existed in physical form.

No one knew why Lucille had decided to do that, especially since Damien had been just a toddler at the time, but we suspected she had transformed because her immense power had become dangerous. Since then, Lucille hadn't made her spectral presence known until the night before I arrived in Nightmare, when Mama had heard her voice. I'd heard Lucille once, too, and even Damien had caught her whisper on the wind.

And, it seemed, Lucille was willing to make her presence known to Lucy in order to help her with her growing psychic abilities.

"What kind of things is Lucille telling you to practice?" I asked.

"She said I should spend more time on the playground. Especially on the swings." Lucy spread her arms and laughed. "I like that kind of practice!"

Lucy had been seeing the ghost of a girl on the playground at school. Recently, we had learned the ghost might be one of the Vanishing Girls, three girls who had left Nightmare Elementary School one day in nineteen fifty-nine and were never seen again. Lucy wanted to help the ghost, and Lucille's guidance could assist with that.

"Have you seen the ghost recently?" I asked.

"Not for a while, but I've been talking to her whenever I'm on the playground, and no one else can hear me. I tell her it's okay to come talk to me, because I'm nice."

"You're very nice," Mama said. She was no longer leaning on the counter and seemed to have recovered from Lucy's news. "And we might just need your help with this murder case, but in the meantime, I'm sure you have some homework to do."

Lucy's shoulders drooped. "Yeah. I'll go get started." She trudged up the stairs, making as much noise and sighing as loudly as possible as she went.

"I'm watching her after school every day this week," Mama explained to Damien. "Mia's booked full at the hair salon, and Nick has been busy. This time of year, tourists on road trips flood his shop, needing all kinds of help with their cars."

"I can't believe my mom is coming to her in dreams," Damien said a bit wistfully. "She's never done that for me."

I wrapped an arm around Damien's waist. "I'm sure she has her reasons."

"Nick and Mia are going to have to know sooner rather than later," Mama said. It was a discussion we'd been having a lot lately. As Lucy's psychic abilities began to develop, there would come a point when her parents would have to be told that the supernatural world existed, and their daughter was a part of it.

"They don't need to know everything just yet," Damien cautioned. Telling them Lucy was psychic was one thing. Introducing them to Nightmare's resident wendigo was another.

"Nick and Mia know Lucille was my sister, of course," Mama continued. "I have the cutest picture of Lucille holding Nick and you, Damien, when you were both tiny little things."

Damien shifted uncomfortably. After Lucille had ceased to exist in human form, Baxter had cut his ties with her family. Damien had grown up not knowing he was related to Mama, and even though Mama said it had been done to keep Lucille's family members safe from supernatural threats, it was still a big loss for Damien. He had grown up feeling isolated and weird, never quite fitting in at the Sanctuary or anywhere else.

"Anyway," Mama continued, "if Lucy suddenly starts

talking about a woman named Lucille in her dreams, Nick is going to realize it's his aunt, even if he doesn't believe she's anything more than a figment of Lucy's imagination."

"I'm sure Nick and Mia will be supportive," I said. Mama looked like she needed reassurance.

"And so will we," Damien added. "My father taught me to suppress my abilities when they began to manifest, and he wouldn't even tell me what I was. I didn't know what he or my mother were, for that matter. All I knew was that I was supernatural and dangerous, and I should hide my abilities. It was a terrible way to grow up. If Lucy's skills are growing this quickly, then she needs her family to help her explore this aspect of herself. She needs their support, and ours."

"Will you two be there with me for the talk with Nick and Mia?" Mama asked. "I know Benny will be willing to come, too, but I'll take all the moral support I can get."

Damien and I readily agreed, and Mama seemed to relax after that. Though, while Damien and I chatted a bit, I could hear her at her desk, occasionally mumbling things such as, "It's like I'm getting my sister back."

Eventually, I sent Damien on his way. I would see him in just a few hours at work, and there was no reason for him to stay at the motel and watch over me. I appreciated his concern for my safety, but I assured him the van wouldn't be showing up again, either in the office or in my apartment. "Unless the van can go up a flight of stairs," I teased.

One of the reasons I had shooed Damien away was so I could get in some quiet time before work. It had been a long, strange day, beginning with Reyes waking me up that morning to tell me about the second murder victim. I needed to put my feet up and tune out the world for a while.

Not surprisingly, kicking my feet up turned into a nice late-afternoon snooze, but at least I'd had the foresight to set my alarm. Soon, I was on my way to the Sanctuary.

I hated driving there again, since it was such perfect weather for walking, but I also knew it was the safer option.

Damien's office was locked when I arrived at the Sanctuary, so I headed for the dining room, instead. That night's pre-work meeting—what I called the family meeting—wouldn't start for another fifteen minutes, but the room was already packed.

I knew why when I looked toward the podium and saw Vivian and Amos standing there, talking to a cluster of people. Nearby, the ghosts of Tanner and McCrory were in a conversation with Gunnar and Malcolm. Everyone had arrived early to say farewell to the group heading east to search for Baxter.

The babble in the room quieted down when Justine stepped up to the podium to begin the meeting. After running through a short list of announcements, she said, "As you all know, Vivian, Amos, Tanner, and McCrory are hitting the road once we wrap up the meeting. Remember, no matter how difficult things seem, and no matter how many miles separate us, we have each other."

"And together, we can face the daylight," everyone in the room said in unison.

I had heard the phrase only once before, and that had been during my first family meeting, when I was just beginning work at the Sanctuary. I had discovered a dead body on the front lawn the previous evening, and the call-and-response seemed to be something this group did to remind each other they could get through anything, no matter how tough.

After the meeting, I made my way up front to wish Vivian and Amos safe travels. I could hug the two of them, but not the ghosts, so I had to make do with giving Tanner and McCrory my most encouraging smile. "I hope the four of you get some answers," I told the ghosts. "But be careful, please."

"I'm always careful," Tanner said.

"Outlaws are the opposite of careful," McCrory said with a sniff. "But I'll look out for him, ma'am."

"By the way," I said, "where does that 'together we can face the daylight' phrase come from?"

Tanner's eyes had taken on a mischievous look when he was teasing about being careful, but he sobered quickly. "Baxter introduced that a long time ago, after a few of our residents had a run-in with a hunter. They all lived, but it was close."

"And, now, it's a way to give each other strength," I said, nodding. "I'll see you two again soon."

The mood at work that night was a bizarre mix of excited and subdued. Between the group hitting the road, the ghouls, and word that a hunter was in town—I didn't know if Damien had said something, or if someone had spotted Robert and made the same inference we did—there was a strange feeling of anticipation in the air.

Luckily, I had been assigned to the lagoon vignette inside the haunt. Pretending to be a pirate and getting to spend time with both Theo and Seraphina, our siren, was a guaranteed way to make me forget about my worries.

Early in the night, between groups coming through our section of the haunted house, Seraphina called my name. When I looked in her direction, I saw her leaning over the top edge of her water tank, which was right next to the prop pirate ship. Her golden hair was shining in the overhead light that let guests see her through the window on the front of the tank.

"I need you to give me the scoop," she said. "Fiona only heard some of the details of what's going on."

I lifted my tricorn pirate hat in a little salute. "As soon as we close tonight, I'll be happy to pass along the gossip. But, I'll warn you, it's not good."

"Life is always exciting for us here, isn't it?" Seraphina glanced over her shoulder at the group of five just coming into the vignette, and with a flash of her silver tail, she disappeared under the water.

As soon as the Sanctuary closed at midnight and the last guests had exited the building, I made good on my promise to Seraphina, filling her in on all the gory details of the past two days. Theo stood next to me, adding comments now and then. Really, though, I thought he was mostly there to creep me out by standing uncomfortably close while wearing his zombie makeup.

"And that's it," I finished. "Mama was right when she said there were some shady characters showing up in Nightmare." I put out a hand to keep Theo from leaning even closer to me. "Don't even think about it."

"Aww," Theo said. One of his favorite things to do was to kiss me on the cheek when he was in his full zombie pirate getup, because he loved how much it disgusted me.

Seraphina shivered, her green-tinted shoulders hitching upward. "You were right about none of it being good. And riding a horse sounds awful."

"Thank you!" *Finally, someone who agrees with me.*

I wished Theo and Seraphina a good night, then made my way to the costume room to change back into my regular clothes. Once I looked like normal Olivia instead of pirate Olivia, I headed for Damien's office, which was down the front hallway in the east wing of the building.

As I was passing through the entryway, I heard a knock on one of the front doors.

"We're closed," I called.

The knock came again, and I figured a guest must have

lost their car key or phone in the darkness of the haunt, and they had come back to retrieve it. I unlocked the door and opened it. "Did you forget—"

Theo's zombie makeup was gross, but it was nothing compared to the face I was staring at now. I had just answered the door for a ghoul.

CHAPTER ELEVEN

I slammed the door, locked it, then stood there, too shocked to move.

Maybe I just imagined it.

Maybe it was just a regular person with a very unfortunate face.

Maybe my—

Another knock interrupted my efforts to explain away what I had just seen. With a gasp, I turned and pelted toward Damien's office. His door was open, and I ran in so quickly I smacked right into one of the oxblood leather chairs in front of Damien's expansive desk.

I pointed in the direction of the entryway as Damien jumped up from his chair. "Ghoul," I wheezed. "At the door."

Damien ran around his desk and past me, and I followed as fast as I could. I was worried he would open the door and confront the ghoul himself, but instead, he rapped on the door to Zach's office. "I need you," he called.

Without waiting for a response, Damien continued into the entryway. The ghoul was knocking again, but Damien ignored it and went down the hallway that led to the dining room.

Fiona, Malcolm, and Gunnar were standing in a group in the hallway.

"You saw a ghost? Here?" Gunnar was asking Fiona as Damien and I came up.

"Right in the middle of the cemetery vignette, a couple hours before we opened tonight," Fiona said. "A woman."

All three of them turned as Damien stopped in front of them with me on his heels. "There's a ghoul knocking on the front door," he announced.

"Then let's see what it wants," Malcolm answered calmly.

"Do you really think that's a good idea?" I asked. At least, that was what I tried to say. I was so out of breath I wasn't sure I was coherent. Between my shock and the running, my breathing was shallow.

Fiona wrapped an arm around my shoulders, seeming to sense my distress. "You're safe, Olivia," she said softly. It was odd to be comforted by a banshee, but I did feel a bit better.

"What's happening?" Zach asked as he ran up to our group. "And who's at the front door?"

"A ghoul," Gunnar answered.

"So let's find out why it's here." Zach began to turn in the direction he had come from.

"You and Malcolm are either brave or crazy," I said.

"They're right," Damien said. "We won't learn anything if we hide in here."

Reluctantly, I followed everyone to the front door. I reminded myself that ghouls moved slowly, and I was surrounded by very powerful friends. Like Fiona had said, I was safe.

Damien unlocked the door, counted to three, then yanked it open. Instead of finding ourselves face-to-face with a ghoul, though, we saw it walking away, its motions jerky and unsteady.

"Guess he got tired of waiting," Fiona quipped.

"Shall we follow?" Malcom asked.

"Maybe that's what it wants." Damien glanced at Malcolm. "It could be another trap."

"I'll fly a short distance ahead of you, so I can see if other ghouls are waiting for us," Gunnar offered.

"I'll grab some food and catch up," Fiona said. She turned and hurried off, her long white gown billowing out behind her. It was the costume she wore in the cemetery vignette, and the dress combined with her long black hair made her look beautifully frightening. However, I doubted it was the most convenient outfit for following a ghoul through the desert, in the dark.

Gunnar spread his wings and lifted off the ground as soon as we got outside, and the rest of us walked along at an easy pace. At least following a ghoul wasn't something that would make me out of breath.

Fiona caught up to us before we had reached the gallows at the crossroads, and she had a bulging tote bag that was packed with food items. She had also changed into a Nightmare Sanctuary hoodie and black leggings, an ensemble that looked much more comfortable for traipsing around town. "I wasn't sure what they like, so I brought bread, potato chips, some celery, and a few apples," she told us.

"It was nice of you to choose some nutritious things for ghouls who are living a healthier lifestyle," Zach joked. He paused, sniffing the air. "I can smell the one we're following, but not any others."

"I also only smell one," Malcolm said. "So far, we're safe."

We walked for so long that even I eventually relaxed. If it weren't for the dead guy we were following, it would have felt like we were simply out for a nice stroll.

After two hours, I was flagging. Even though we weren't walking quickly, I was exhausted after such a long day, and I was ready for bed. The ghoul, however, was still shuffling along, and it was obvious he was heading in the direction of the state park.

Eventually, Damien took my hand. "You're going to bed."

I protested, but Fiona and Malcolm stepped in to take Damien's side. I would have continued arguing, but Damien looked at me seriously and said, "I don't know what tomorrow will bring, but we're going to need you to be well-rested and ready for some sleuthing."

Instead of walking home alone, which we all agreed was too risky, I called Justine to pick me up in her car. She was more than happy to do so, since it meant I could fill her in on the Sanctuary's surprise visitor and our very slow chase.

I finished bringing Justine up to date as she pulled her car to a stop at the bottom of the stairs leading to my apartment, and she looked at me thoughtfully. "If the ghouls are getting bold enough to wander all the way to the Sanctuary, then people are going to notice. Tourists will explain them away, thinking they're part of the show here, or one of the costumed actors working around High Noon Boulevard. But all it's going to take is for one hunter to spot a ghoul before this town is crawling with more hunters."

"There's already a hunter in town," I reminded Justine. "Jeff's friend."

"Then let's hope more of Jeff's friends don't come for a visit."

I heartily agreed, thanked Justine for the ride, then trudged up my stairs. I was too tired to worry about ghouls or hunters, and I slept soundly until I woke up with my alarm clock the next morning. As I drank my first cup of coffee, I stared out the window at the pristine blue sky outside, thinking over Justine's words about hunters.

I needed to talk to Robert, the hunter who claimed he

was only in town to see his old friend Jeff. I wasn't even sure what I would say to him, but I just had the feeling that we should have a chat.

Since I didn't have a direct way to reach Robert, I called The Lusty Lunch Counter and asked for Jeff. When the call was transferred to his office, I quickly told him about the ghoul who had come to the Sanctuary's front doors the night before.

Jeff did not take the news well. "It had to walk clear across town to get to the haunted house," he pointed out. "Do you know how many people might have spotted it? Worse, someone might have gotten in its way, and the ghoul would have hurt them."

"How do ghouls hurt people, anyway?" I asked. I still hadn't figured that part out.

"They might not be coordinated, but they are strong. If one of them gets its hands around your neck..." Jeff trailed off, then blew out a breath. "I don't like whatever it is that's going on. It's dangerous."

"Agreed. And I'm hoping to have a chat with your friend Robert about the situation. I know you're retired, but Robert isn't. A lot of my friends at the Sanctuary are understandably leery of hunters, so I thought Robert could meet Damien and me somewhere that's free of supernatural creatures."

Except Damien and me, I added silently.

Jeff sighed. "I came to Nightmare to leave hunting behind."

"I know. Which is why I'm not asking you to help beyond setting up a meeting."

Despite some grumbling about just wanting to run his diner in peace and quiet, Jeff did agree to pass along a message to Robert. I asked that Robert meet me at The Caffeinated Cadaver at ten thirty, then thanked Jeff profusely.

As soon as I was off the phone with Jeff, I called Damien, both to ask him to come with me to the coffee shop and to find out what I had missed the night before. All I knew was that everyone was safe, because I had woken up to a text from Damien saying they gave up the chase at three o'clock that morning.

Damien was still half-asleep when he answered the phone, but he agreed to meet me at the coffee shop. He didn't have much to report about the ghoul, though. Damien said it had reached the area where both bodies had been found, then stopped moving.

"I don't know what it wanted at the Sanctuary, but when we wouldn't let it inside, I guess it just went home to the woods," Damien said. He yawned, then ended the call by saying, "I'll see you soon, and I'll be ordering the largest coffee they have."

In a short while, I was on the way to the coffee shop, dressed in jeans, a white blouse, and a lightweight mauve cardigan. Even though it was sunny, there was just a hint of a chill in the light breeze. It was the perfect weather for walking, especially when my route took me right up High Noon Boulevard. The street's buildings had the tall wooden facades that Wild West movies had made so iconic, and there was a covered boardwalk on each side of the street. Between them, the asphalt had been covered with a layer of dirt to add to the old-fashioned look.

If our meeting with Robert went long enough, we'd emerge from the coffee shop at noon, just in time to catch the day's first show from the actors who re-created the shootout between Tanner and McCrory.

The Caffeinated Cadaver was a cozy little coffee shop filled with shabby, overstuffed chairs and plenty of sunshine from the front windows. Its name was a reminder that the space had once been where Nightmare's undertaker did his work. The shop's logo featured a skeleton in a cowboy hat, a steaming cup of coffee in one bony hand.

I was the first to arrive, so I ordered a large coffee for Damien and a latte for myself. By the time I had settled into a chair at a small round table, Robert had arrived. He skipped getting anything to drink and sat down next to me.

"Is it safe to talk here?" he asked, looking around.

There was no one sitting nearby, which meant we wouldn't be overheard. However, I suspected that wasn't what Robert had meant. "I purposely picked a place full of normal, not-at-all-supernatural tourists. You're fine."

Robert's jaw clenched, and he gazed around the room with narrowed eyes. He spotted Damien walking toward us, then turned to me. "No supernaturals, with the exception of you two."

I shrugged. "We can't help what we are." I had to wonder how Robert knew Damien and I were supernatural, since we looked like plain-old humans. Had Jeff somehow learned about the two of us, or had Robert made an assumption?

That was a question for later. In the meantime, there were more important things to discuss.

"You know about the ghouls," I said bluntly. Because, I was certain, there was no way a hunter hadn't noticed reanimated corpses shuffling around town.

Robert nodded briefly, his eyes hardening. "I saw one, last night. It was walking north along a side road. I wanted to follow, but Jeff told me I was just imagining things. He said it was probably a drunk guy stumbling home from the saloon."

"It was walking north?" Damien asked as he slid into the empty chair at our table. "That means you saw it on its way to the Sanctuary. It walked right up to the front doors and knocked."

Robert leaned forward. "You killed it, right?"

"No. We followed it, right back to the state park where two bodies have shown up in the past few days."

Robert was shaking his head. "Don't tell me your little group here is so sweet and kind that you won't even kill a ghoul."

"It had nothing to do with us being nice," Damien said stiffly. "We're trying to learn why they're here, and following it seemed like a smarter idea than killing it."

Robert snorted. "It's obvious what they're doing. Ghouls are often used as sentinels. There's something out there that they're guarding."

CHAPTER TWELVE

Damien and I glanced at each other. We had speculated the ghouls were acting as walking-dead security guards, but hearing Robert say it with such confidence was a surprise.

"Are you sure?" I asked. "How do you know ghouls are often used as sentries?"

Robert waved a hand. "I encountered them when I was trying to get to a closely guarded werewolf once. Another time, they were keeping watch over a witch who was doing revenge spells for people in her town. Then there was the vampire enclave in Baton Rouge…"

"You have a lot of firsthand experience with ghouls, then," I said. "Do you think they're here in Nightmare to keep an eye on something valuable?"

"Valuable, or dangerous." Robert chewed his lip slowly, probably trying to decide if he wanted to investigate what, exactly, the ghouls were guarding. "Did you wait until dawn to see where the ghoul went?"

Damien shook his head. "It was just standing in one spot. We gave up around three o'clock this morning."

"Rookie mistake. Those ghouls are likely going into hiding during the day. Otherwise, people hiking and riding along the trails would see them. They probably go into hiding at dawn, and the ghoul might have led you right to whatever it's guarding."

Damien looked annoyed, but I wasn't sure if it was with himself for not realizing that or with Robert, who was giving Damien a superior look. "We'll be sure to do that the next time one shows up on our doorstep," Damien said stiffly.

"It's possible the ghouls aren't going into hiding," I pointed out. "Because if they are guarding something, it would need to be kept safe during the daylight hours, too. Maybe people have seen the ghouls around but figured they were just hikers."

"Sure, hikers with rotting skin." Robert had an expression on his face that said he thought I was slightly stupid.

"Do you know a guy named Culver, by any chance? Or a Vincent?" I asked, wanting to move on to a new subject.

Robert's expression quickly changed, and his fists clenched. "Jimmy Culver and Vincent Lakehall. I don't know them, but I know who they are. They're notorious magicians. They're in Nightmare, too?"

"One of them, Vincent, is the second murder victim," I said. Before I could continue, I spotted someone walking toward us and looked up to see Jeff.

"Just checking in to make sure everyone is playing nice," he said. Even though he was saying it jokingly, I could tell by his stance that he was worried our meeting might have gone off the rails.

"Culver and Lakehall are in town," Robert muttered. "Though, according to Olivia here, Lakehall is dead. It was his body the police found on the trail yesterday morning."

Jeff shook his head. "Those two are bad news. I can't say I'm sorry to know one of them is gone."

"Vincent was murdered," I continued, "and Jimmy Culver was nearly run over by a van yesterday."

Jeff let out a strained laugh. "Why do vans keep popping up in murder investigations?" He was referring to a murder case in which he had helped catch the killer, but in that instance, the people with the van wound up being helpful rather than murderous.

"Who was driving the van?" Robert asked.

I shrugged. "An older guy. Gray hair that was a bit long. I'd never seen him before."

"I know a lot of guys who look like that," Robert pointed out.

Jeff grabbed a nearby chair and dragged it to our table. As he plopped down, he said, "What do you mean you'd never seen him before? Were you there when Culver was almost run over?"

I nodded. "We were in the parking lot of Cowboy's Corral."

"Magicians can be trouble," Jeff warned. "Especially ones who believe their own hype. You keep your distance from Culver, and you tell me if anything else happens with him. Robert and I will try to keep an eye out, too." Jeff sat back in his chair and sighed. "I'm supposed to be retired."

"We know," Damien said. "We aren't asking for your help, just your knowledge. Robert has already been very helpful, especially with getting more insight into Nightmare's ghoul problem."

"You may not be asking for help," Jeff said, "but neither one of us wants to sit back and let ghouls roam unchecked."

Damien raised both hands. "We will deal with them, I promise. In the meantime, we'll be keeping watch in the hopes of learning something more about what they're guarding."

Jeff got an odd look on his face. He opened his mouth to speak, then glanced quickly at Robert before closing it again.

He knows exactly what Damien and I are thinking, I realized. *And he doesn't want his friend to catch on.*

Robert stood. "Good luck. We'll give you space to learn what you can from the ghouls, but if you take too long, I won't hesitate to take care of them myself."

"Understood," Damien answered.

Jeff and Robert left, leaving Damien and me to look at each other. "Did I make a mistake telling Robert about the ghouls?" I whispered. The longer the meeting had gone on, the more I had felt like a weight was pressing down on my ribcage.

"Robert already knew about them," Damien said. He took my hand and squeezed it. "He said he *thought* he saw one last night, but he knew exactly what it was walking along the road. Hunters know the difference between a ghoul and a drunk person."

I nodded slowly. "And Jeff probably asked him to leave the matter alone, because he didn't want to get dragged into some kind of supernatural drama."

"That's what I assume. So, no, I don't think you made a mistake. Robert learned nothing from us, except perhaps that two magicians came to town, and one wound up dead. But he gave us far more information in return, because we now know Culver and Lakehall are part of the supernatural community."

"Which means Culver might know something about the ghouls."

"Yes, but there's something more important than the ghouls that you and I need to discuss first." Damien glanced around, then said, "Let's head downstairs."

I laughed. "Under the Undertaker's isn't open yet. It's not even noon!" I wasn't sure what time the supernatural bar opened, but I was pretty sure it wasn't in the morning.

"No, but someone will be there, so we can get in. I don't care if a fairy overhears us, but I don't want to risk anyone here listening in."

We grabbed our coffees and walked out of The

Caffeinated Cadaver, then headed along the boardwalk until we could turn and skirt around to the backside of the row of buildings that housed the coffee shop. Damien went straight to a metal door in the alley and knocked loudly.

We had to wait about a minute before the small window in the door slid open, and a pair of violet-colored eyes peered at us. "We're closed! Oh! Damien Shackleford, what are you doing here at this hour? Never mind. Come inside."

The window slid shut with a snap, then the door opened to reveal a slender fairy with long silvery hair and high cheekbones. I recognized her as Clara's aunt as she waved us inside.

When the door had been shut and locked behind us, she said, "What's wrong?"

"We're not sure, but have you heard that ghouls have been spotted in Nightmare?" Damien asked.

"Clara told us."

"And there's a hunter in town, though he claims he's here just to visit a friend. Olivia and I have something to discuss, and this seemed like a safe place to talk."

Clara's aunt gestured toward the spiral staircase that led into the basement underneath the coffee shop. "Head on down. I see you brought coffee with you, but if you decide you want something stronger, you just holler."

Soon, Damien and I were sitting on low stools set between long jewel-toned strips of fabric that hung from the ceiling. Under the Undertaker's was elegant when the candles throughout the space were the only illumination, but at the moment, the overhead lights were on. Dozens of wine and martini glasses were lined up on the bar, and I suspected we had interrupted a bit of reorganizing.

"We have no reason to doubt Robert's statement that the ghouls are likely guarding something," Damien said.

"It would explain why the ghouls are mostly sticking to one general area of the state park."

"You think they're guarding Baxter," I said without hesitation. It had been my first thought when Robert said ghouls were often used as sentries, and I knew from the look Damien had given me in the coffee shop that his mind had made the same connection.

"And, if they are, can we get to him before Robert or some other hunter does?"

"A hunter or a magician." I sighed. "What do we do now?"

"Keep watching. And look for the exact place the ghouls are guarding. We don't know for sure my father is still here in Nightmare, so we won't call Vivian and Amos off their hunt on the East Coast just yet."

"How could Baxter still be in Nightmare? The witches did a locator spell for him on nearly the same spot where we found the dead ghoul, and they got nothing."

"Maybe he isn't still in town. Whether he is or not, though, those ghouls are keeping guard over something. Anyone who would use ghouls is not a good person, which means whatever they're guarding is likely dangerous. We don't want it in the hands of someone with bad intentions."

Damien's chest was rising and falling rapidly, and I pressed a palm against the front of his dark-gray button-down shirt. "We're going to find your dad," I told him firmly.

"I hope so." Damien's lips pressed into a thin line, and I pulled him into a tight hug. The idea that Baxter might be just a few miles outside of town was probably making his absence even harder for Damien. Baxter could be so close, but we still didn't know how to find him.

We hugged for a long time, but eventually, Damien sat back. "Come on. We won't accomplish anything sitting down here, and I think we need to warn Mama that one of her guests is a magician. I'll drive you home, and we can go into the motel office and chat with her.

After thanking Clara's aunt profusely for letting us use Under the Undertaker's, we left and went straight to the front office of Cowboy's Corral. Not only was Mama there, sitting at her desk, but so was Lucy. She was shoveling a peanut butter and jelly sandwich into her mouth.

"You should be in school," I told her.

Lucy shrugged. "Iffa got ma lunsh," she said as she chewed.

I looked at Mama for an interpretation. "She forgot her lunch, and she didn't have any money to buy one, so she called me. I could have dropped a lunch off for her, but she had enough time for me to pick her up and bring her here for a bit."

"In that case," Damien said, "I'd be happy to drive Lucy back to school while you and Olivia have a chat."

In other words, Lucy shouldn't be anywhere near our conversation about ghouls, magicians, and murder.

Mama's eyebrows slowly lifted, and she nodded.

Lucy must have swallowed the rest of her sandwich, because when she spoke again, I could understand her.

"She says what's underneath is what you seek."

CHAPTER THIRTEEN

"Lucy, who says that what we seek is underneath?" I asked, even though I already knew the answer.

"The nice lady with my name." Lucy smiled happily. "My…" She looked at Mama questioningly.

"Great-aunt," Mama supplied. She was talking to Lucy, but her eyes were darting around the office, like she might catch a glimpse of her sister. "You said you've dreamed about Lucille. Is this the first time she's communicated with you while you're awake?"

"Yeah. Pretty cool, right?" Lucy lifted a gooey chocolate chip cookie to her lips and took a big bite.

"'What's underneath is what you seek.' We're seeking my father, and, of course, she wants to help us find him." Damien stopped and swallowed hard.

"So, he's underneath something?" I asked. "Or, is this more of a metaphorical message?"

"Maybe…" Damien began.

"Maybe, what?" Mama prompted.

When Damien spoke again, his voice was nearly inaudible. "Maybe my father is underneath the watch of…" He glanced in Lucy's direction, then raised both arms and wobbled them.

I couldn't help my laugh at Damien's impression of a ghoul.

"I would really like to have a chat with Culver again," I said. "I know Jeff and Robert warned me to steer clear, but Culver might know something. It can't be a coincidence that Vincent Lakehall wound up murdered out there where the"—I raised my arms like Damien had—"are wandering around."

"I agree," Damien said.

Mama pointed at Damien. "Lucy needs to get back to school. Can you take her?" Then, she pointed at me. "And you need to fill me in, because this is the first mention I've heard of Baxter being tangled up in all of this."

"It's just speculation," I said quickly. I didn't want to give Mama false hope that we were close to finding her brother-in-law.

"Lucy, are you ready to go?" Damien asked. "I'll drop you off at school before I head to the Sanctuary."

Lucy hopped up, brushed a few crumbs from her pink shirt, and blew a kiss toward Mama and me. As she followed Damien out the door, I heard her ask, "Can we go really fast in your car?"

I shook my head. "She's fearless. Lucille just spoke to her, in her mind, and instead of being unsettled by it, she wants to pretend she's a race car driver on her way back to school."

"Lucille was the same way." Mama took me by the arm and pulled me to one of the chairs, then sat down in the one next to it. "Now, what did you and Damien come here to tell me?"

I filled Mama in on the latest news, including that Culver was a magician, and she should keep an extra-close watch on him.

"Magicians," Mama muttered.

"Jeff and Robert had the same reaction. What is a magician, and why are they so despised?"

"Magicians use magic, but in a different way than

witches. Instead of potions or spells, magicians prefer using darker methods. They'll tap into a person's energy to grow their power, for instance."

"That sounds unpleasant."

"At best, it leaves the person exhausted. At worst, they die." Mama shook her head. "And if those two came to Nightmare in search of Baxter, well, you can imagine that having a captive phoenix would give them enormous power. They could drain him of his energy again and again, but Baxter would be reborn each time."

"An endless battery," I murmured.

"Exactly. And, to make things even more complicated, Lucille is giving us cryptic messages."

"At least she's trying to help," I said.

Mama had been looking worried, her brow furrowed and her mouth turned down. Suddenly, though, she gave me a sly smile. "I don't think it's a coincidence that Lucille spoke to Lucy after you and Damien had arrived. Somehow, the three of you are all giving Lucille strength. I think that's why she seems to be waking up after years of silence."

I nodded slowly. "Lucy's growing psychic abilities, my growing conjuring abilities, and Damien's growing power —whatever it is the child of a phoenix and a psychic can do—is all helping Lucille. Like you just said about magicians using a person's energy to grow their own power, maybe we're acting like batteries for Lucille."

"I think so. We knew you and Damien were going to be powerful together, and now that there's another psychic in the family, Lucille is growing stronger. She's joining the search for Baxter."

"The more, the merrier."

Mama chuckled darkly. "It is definitely time for that talk with Nick and Mia."

I couldn't argue with that.

The rest of the day passed slowly, in part because nothing having to do with magic or murder happened. I went back to my apartment to make a sandwich for lunch, and I got some marketing work done for Cowboy's Corral. The highlight of the afternoon was going back to the motel office with my laptop, so I was there when Lucy came bounding through the door after school.

While I knew Lucille was still fresh on both my brain and Mama's, Lucy was full of stories about her day at school and all her friends there. It was refreshing, actually. No matter what kind of bizarre drama we had stumbled into with the ghouls and the murders, most people in Nightmare were still going about their lives. Eventually, we would get Baxter back, and the lives of everyone at the Sanctuary would go back to normal, too.

Damien texted halfway through the afternoon to say another watch party would be heading out after the Sanctuary closed that night. He had followed that news up with a suggestion I grab a quick nap, followed by an emoji of a winking face.

He knew me so well.

I squeezed in an hour-long snooze, knowing this time we would want to stay on the hunt until dawn to follow any ghoul we could find to its daytime hideout. I tended not to like advice that resulted in me losing sleep, but Robert had made a good point that if there weren't reports of the walking dead coming in, then the ghouls must be hiding somewhere during the day.

When I walked into the dining room at work that night, I saw the three witches sitting at one side of a table. Across from them were Mori, Fiona, Theo, and Damien. Gunnar was standing to one side, and Seraphina was parked nearby in her mobile water tank. She had maneuvered so she could fold her arms on the edge of the barrel-sized tank, and she was leaning toward the group, looking worried.

"We should do shifts," Mori was saying as I walked up, then she raised her hand to stifle a yawn. "Sorry. I slept terribly."

"I think that's a great idea," Fiona agreed instantly. "There's no point in all of us being out there for the entire night."

"May I make a suggestion?" Seraphina asked. "I know I can't go out and search with you, but I can stay here to help coordinate. I think, instead of having two shifts of people out there on the trails, we should have two search parties. One on the trails, and one in town, looking for the van that nearly ran over Olivia. A couple of us will stay here to relay messages."

I raised my eyebrows as I squeezed onto the end of the bench next to Morgan, the eldest witch. "That's not a bad idea," I said.

"I can do surveillance from the air again," Gunnar said, nodding. "And I can help keep Seraphina apprised of where everyone is and what's happening."

"Fiona, why don't you and I take the van search?" Mori suggested. "The two of us can pass for regular humans, and I can grab a snack from a tourist while we're out searching."

Fiona quickly agreed to the plan, and I gave her and Mori a description of the van while Damien added in details about it that I'd missed, like the gold-flake pinstriping above the wheels.

"Guess I was too busy trying not to die to notice that," I quipped.

"I was busy, too," Damien said, pretending to be offended. "I helped you not die."

"We've got two murders, an attempted murder, and plenty of suspects to go around," Gunnar said. "What

97

would be nice is if we had a lead on who made the ghouls and put them on guard in the first place."

Beside me, I felt Morgan's frail body shake as she began to cackle. "Oh, that's easy!"

"We should have thought of it ourselves," Madge said. She flashed a brilliant smile at Gunnar. "Thank you for the suggestion."

"But I haven't suggested—"

"We'll do it tonight!" Maida broke in excitedly.

"Our locator spell failed to find Baxter," Morgan said, "but we can try it again to locate the resurrectionist responsible for the ghouls."

"That's a great idea," Gunnar said. "But don't you need a personal item from the person you're using the locator spell on?"

"All we need is a ghoul to go by," Morgan assured him.

"Excellent," I said. "Then maybe we won't have to stay up all night watching the trails. But how do you catch a ghoul, anyway?"

CHAPTER FOURTEEN

I had expected the witches to explain how we were going to catch a ghoul for their locator spell. Instead, it was Fiona who piped up. "Catching a ghoul will be easy! Even the dead can't resist the siren's call."

Everyone turned and looked at Seraphina, who appeared simultaneously flattered and horrified. "You want to take me out to the state park?" She tilted her head toward the surface of the water in her tank. "I'm not exactly built for hiking."

"We'll manage," Fiona assured her.

Seraphina rolled her eyes. "I liked the plan where I was going to stay right here, acting as the coordinator for all of you."

The witches declared they would prepare everything necessary for the spell as soon as the Sanctuary closed that night, then they would accompany us to the state park. Once Seraphina had lured a ghoul to us, they would quickly do the locator spell, so we could find out where the resurrectionist was before any more ghouls could respond to the siren's call.

It sounded dangerous, but at the same time, I liked the idea. We would get a lot more answers if we could find the person responsible for the ghouls and go have a talk with them, rather than waiting up all night in the hopes of following a ghoul to whatever they were guarding.

"I'll get in the kitchen right after work and load up on food, in case we get overwhelmed by ghouls," I said.

"No," Theo said quickly. "I don't think you should go, Olivia. You're right that Seraphina might bring more ghouls than we want to the party, and we can't risk you getting hurt. Or worse."

I frowned. "All of you are going to risk it. Why shouldn't I?"

Theo pointed at himself. "Mori and I are vampires. Fiona is a banshee. We're hard to kill."

"So is Olivia," Damien spoke up. He looked at me proudly. "She was able to conjure her safety when that van nearly ran her down."

"We did that together," I pointed out.

"Then I guess I'm coming with you tonight."

Theo looked like he wanted to protest, but he took one look at the determination on Damien's face and simply shrugged. I appreciated that my friends were concerned about my safety, but there was no way I was going to stay behind.

"What are we plotting?" Justine asked. She had just walked up to our table, a clipboard in one hand. "Whatever it is, I want in."

"Me, too," said Clara, who appeared at her elbow.

"We have a job opening here at headquarters," Seraphina said. "I was going to do it, but Fi recruited me for field duty."

"Great," Justine said. "I have no idea what we're getting ourselves into, but it's time for the meeting, so you can fill me in later."

It was difficult to concentrate on anything Justine said during the family meeting. I was excited about our outing later, and while work normally seemed to pass quickly because I enjoyed it so much, I anticipated a long evening ahead.

Justine announced I would be posted at the front that night, taking tickets and ushering guests into the queue that snaked back and forth inside the entryway. It was one of my usual posts, and as much as I enjoyed playing a scary pirate in the lagoon vignette, I also liked getting to greet guests and see their excitement as they entered the building.

As it turned out, the night was very long for me, but not because of my eagerness to get out to the state park and watch the witches do their spell. Instead, I found myself looking at every face that went past as I tore tickets. I was looking for signs the person might be dead already.

Of course, not one single guest was a rotting corpse, but answering the door for a ghoul on Tuesday night had made me a little nervous about standing at the front doors for four hours.

I was also keeping an eye out for an older man with lank gray hair, just in case the mysterious van man came back to finish the job.

I quite literally jumped when a hand landed on my shoulder halfway through the night. I yelped and whirled around while the group that had just walked up to me laughed.

It was Malcolm, and I saw he was trying to hold back his own laughter. "It's your break time," he told me. "And, by the way, count me in for tonight's excursion, too."

My heart was beating faster than usual, but I also felt relief. "When Theo called it a party, he wasn't kidding. We're going to have a big group out there tonight."

Malcolm leaned down to whisper in my ear, so the guests wouldn't overhear. "We want there to be more of us than there are of them." He straightened up, then turned his attention to the three people crowded in the doorway and gave them a grin that looked downright sinister. "Now, which one of you will be the next to scream tonight?"

As I was heading for the dining room to have a snack and a bit of a rest, I heard the woman in the group Malcolm had just addressed giggling nervously. I looked over my shoulder to see her holding her ticket toward Malcolm while also leaning back as far as possible from him.

Yeah, I'll be perfectly safe tonight if Malcolm is with us.

When the last guests entered shortly before midnight, I closed the door and locked up. I had seen Zach all night long as he sat in the ticket window, but he had been too far away for me to talk to, so I headed to his office. When I went in, he was just closing the ticket window, which looked out over the area covered by the building's portico.

"Are you joining us tonight?" I asked.

Zach shook his head. "No, I'm staying here. We don't want to leave the Sanctuary unprotected, so I'll hold down the fort with Justine and Clara." Zach pulled double duty as the Sanctuary's accountant and security guard, with the exception of the three days a month he was a wolf.

"Good plan. I'll see you in the dining room shortly, then."

I was the first of our group to reach the dining room, since I didn't have to change out of a costume. Felipe was in there, and he trotted up to me, tail wagging. I was scratching him behind the ears when Damien came in. He had been dressed in a suit, as usual, but he had swapped his jacket and pants for a pair of black jeans and a button-down shirt with the sleeves rolled up.

"You look awfully nice for ghoul hunting," I commented.

Damien sat down next to me, gave me a kiss, then rubbed Felipe's snout. "I didn't bring my grungy ghoul-hunting clothes with me tonight," he noted.

Before long, we had been joined by all the others who were going to be a part of the search. Seraphina was going with us, which meant Fiona would be, too, since we would need both her van and her expertise at transporting a siren around town.

Because Fiona wouldn't be joining Mori in the hunt for the van man, after all, Theo had volunteered to help out with that search. Zach, Justine, and Clara would be staying at the Sanctuary, and Gunnar would be flying overhead.

That left Damien, Malcolm, and me, plus the witches, Seraphina, and Fiona. Vivian had said she sensed six ghouls when she had visited the state park, so we would hopefully outnumber them, exactly as Malcolm had planned.

Except, I realized, the numbers weren't what mattered. I was heading out with seven incredibly powerful supernatural creatures. Besides, if things got really dangerous, we could run a lot faster than any of the ghouls.

Before Seraphina could lure a ghoul for us, we had to get her to the state park. It was easy to load her up at the Sanctuary: Fiona had procured a van when she brought Seraphina across the country to take refuge at the Sanctuary, and she had a makeshift ramp that let her wheel Seraphina's mobile water tank right into it.

"For the record," Fiona said as she closed the back doors, "I've never tried to kill anyone with *my* van."

Malcolm got into the passenger seat while the rest of us climbed into the side door of the van. There were no seats, so we all settled onto the floor around Seraphina. Every time Fiona hit a bump or took a curve too fast, water would splash out of Seraphina's tank. Maida thought it was hilarious whenever one of us got doused, and she giggled most of the drive.

As soon as we reached the parking lot of the state park,

though, she sobered. All of us fell quiet, as if the gravity of what we were attempting to do had finally hit us.

Malcolm and Damien got the ramp out and rolled Seraphina out of the van, then wheeled her into position right at the edge of the parking lot. Taking her down one of the trails was out of the question, and Fiona even mused that she needed to build an off-road version of the tank for the future.

"No," Seraphina said firmly. "Like I said, I'm not built for hiking. I'm happy staying home and looking at pretty pictures of trees and rocks."

The witches quickly set up a map of Nightmare on one of the picnic tables and placed a lantern next to it, then laid out the other items for the locator spell. At a nod from Morgan, Seraphina began to sing while the rest of us clamped our hands over our ears, with the exception of the witches, who were apparently immune to the siren's song.

Even the muffled sound of Seraphina's singing was beautiful, but it was also incredibly loud. As she sang, the rest of us kept an alert watch for anyone responding to her call.

There was slight movement on one of the trails, and I looked to see a ghoul slowly moving toward us. Seraphina continued singing until the ghoul passed close to the picnic table, where the witches stood ready.

Even with my hands still over my ears, I could hear Madge's gagging noises as she reached out and put a hand on the ghoul's back. Maida and Morgan quickly got to work with the bowls, creating the magical mixture on top of the map.

We all dropped our hands from our ears and watched in silence as the same kind of snake-like form began to slither across the map.

Before, the snake had slid right over the edge of the

picnic table. This time, its head raised slightly, then fell down onto the map, unmoving.

"Right there!" Morgan announced.

I moved closer to the table and saw that when the magical snake had dropped onto the map, it had landed with its tongue out. The long, thin line ended at a spot along the main road through Nightmare.

"Oh," Madge said.

"Interesting," Maida added.

I leaned closer, my eyes narrowed.

The snake's tongue was pointed right at Cowboy's Corral.

CHAPTER FIFTEEN

Madge had let go of the ghoul, and she wiped her hand on her flower-print dress. "I've had to touch some gross things for spells before, but this is the worst."

The ghoul stood quietly by, and I quickly turned my attention back to the map. "The resurrectionist is staying at Cowboy's Corral?" I asked incredulously.

"Looks like Culver might be more than just a magician," Damien said.

"If Culver made these ghouls, then does that mean he killed Vincent Lakehall? He was probably telling me the truth when he said he and Lakehall got into a fight, and we already had him on our suspect list."

Damien shook his head. "Speculation won't get us anywhere. We need to talk to Culver again."

"I'll go knock on his door first thing in the morning," I promised.

"Why wait?" Malcolm asked. "If the resurrectionist is this man staying at the motel, let's go talk to him now. He probably keeps nocturnal hours, like most of us."

"Okay," I agreed. "But in the meantime, what do we do about them?" I pointed toward the area where several trails began. Two more ghouls were walking toward us.

"We pack up very quickly," Fiona said. She was already heading for Seraphina's tank.

In the time it took us to get everyone and everything back into the van, the ghouls had only advanced about twenty feet. Even still, the tires of the van screeched as Fiona peeled out of the parking lot, giving me flashbacks to the attack on Culver at the motel and sending water from Seraphina's tank flying.

When we got to the motel, Fiona pulled into a parking spot, and Malcolm began to open the passenger door.

"Wait," I cautioned. "Maybe we shouldn't all go. We don't want to scare Culver, or make him feel threatened."

"Why not?" Malcolm asked, sounding slightly disappointed.

"Because we're nicer than that," Damien pointed out.

"I suppose."

"Olivia and I will go talk to him," Damien continued. "The rest of you stay here, but be ready to spring into action if it looks like there might be trouble."

"We just have one problem," I pointed out. "I'm not entirely sure which room Culver is staying in. I only saw the general direction he came from." I turned toward the witches. "Ladies, can you do a locator spell to pin down the exact room?"

All three of them were shaking their heads before I finished asking my question. "We didn't bring the ghoul with us," Madge pointed out.

Oh, right.

Damien and I quietly got out of the van, hoping not to disturb anyone staying at the motel. We were heading in the direction of the area I knew Culver was staying in when I said, "Mama is going to lecture me if I knock on the wrong door and wake up her guests."

"You can conjure knocking on the correct door," Damien suggested. "What you want most right now is to get some answers from Culver. Focus on that desire, and let it lead you to the right room."

I closed my eyes, took a few deep breaths, and pictured Culver's face in my mind. "I want answers from you," I murmured. "I need to talk to the resurrectionist."

I was saying those words for the third time when I heard Malcolm hissing Damien's name. We both turned to see Malcolm standing about ten feet away, and instead of saying anything, he simply pointed.

A van was slowly rolling through the parking lot. It was driving down the side of the lot where my apartment was, and soon, it would make the turn to come down the side where Culver's room was, which meant it would pass right by Damien and me.

The van made the turn, and as it got closer to us, Malcolm smoothly stepped right into its path.

I opened my mouth to shout and began to jump forward, but Damien wrapped an arm around my waist. "He'll be okay," he said quickly.

In other words, I thought, *don't conjure. Let Malcolm do whatever it is he's trying to do.*

The van came to an abrupt halt, just inches from Malcolm, who was staring at the driver placidly.

A moment later, the van began to back up, but the motion quickly stopped. I craned my head and could just see the edge of Fiona's body. She was standing behind the van. The driver had nowhere to go, unless he was willing to drive over Fiona or Malcolm.

Having encountered the van driver before, I expected he wouldn't care about plowing over either one of them. I was surprised, then, when the driver rolled down his window and stuck his head out of it. "Get out of the way!" he shouted at Malcolm. "Are you trying to get yourself run over?"

"Not at all," Malcom assured him calmly. "We're simply trying to get some information. For starters, what are you doing driving through the motel at this hour?"

"That's none of your business," the driver spat.

"As a matter of fact, it is our business. Don't you wonder what we're doing here at this hour, too? I expect all of us are here for the same person: Jimmy Culver, the magician."

The driver gaped at Malcolm. He grunted, then said, "I don't know who you're talking about."

"The man you tried to kill a couple days ago," I said, raising my voice loud enough for the driver to hear me. "You nearly killed me, too."

"You two were standing in the middle of the parking lot. I was just trying to get past."

"Sure," I answered in a flat tone.

"Do you only go after living people?" Malcolm asked. "Or did you kill the ghoul out at the state park, too?"

The driver's face grew longer as his mouth dropped open. For a moment, he couldn't say anything. "How do you...? Never mind. Get out of my way. I just want to leave."

Malcolm glanced at Damien, who said, "Let him go."

With a shrug, Malcolm sidestepped so he was just out of the path of the van. The driver pulled his head back inside the window, and soon, the van was rolling away, toward the exit of the parking lot.

"We didn't get anything from him," Malcolm commented.

"What were we supposed to do, throw him in the basement and keep him prisoner until he talked?" Damien asked.

Malcolm looked like he thought that wasn't a terrible idea, but he sighed. "You're right. We're not the monsters."

Damien's hand slid into mine, then he turned so he could look at my face. "You're shaking," he said.

"Am I?" I bounced on the balls of my feet, trying to get

rid of my jitters. "I guess seeing that van again brought back some bad memories."

Damien glanced at the north wing of the motel, then back at me. "We'll wait until tomorrow to talk to Culver. We've had enough excitement for one night."

"Also, we need to reconsider what we're going to say to Culver," I noted. "We assumed the witches' spell was identifying him as the resurrectionist, but what if the van driver has been doing laps through here all night?"

Malcolm had stepped up to us, and he said, "The van could have been driving through here at the very moment the spell was completed."

"And I was trying to conjure a conversation with the resurrectionist at the moment Malcolm spotted the van," I added.

"Either way," Damien pointed out, "Culver is somehow involved in all of this."

"Agreed," I said. "And I'll ask him all about it tomorrow morning."

"Not without me." Damien's voice was firm.

"Or me," Malcolm said. "We'll come to your apartment in the morning, and we can all go talk to Culver together."

"In the meantime, I'll walk you home." Damien offered his arm to me, and I took it as I laughed.

"It's a long way," I warned him.

"It's worth it to keep you safe."

It would have been nice if Damien could have stayed for a bit once we reached my apartment. After seeing the ghouls and finding out the resurrectionist was either staying in the same place I lived, or driving laps around it, I could have used a little quiet time with Damien to settle my nerves.

Plus, he was still looking awfully good, despite the

many times he'd been splashed during the drive. I hated to let that view go so soon.

Our friends were waiting in the van, though, so I said goodnight to Damien fairly quickly, and in a few minutes, I was on my own and in bed.

I was awakened in the morning by the sound of knocking. I rolled over and checked the time. "Really, guys?" I mumbled as I climbed out of bed. Neither Damien nor Malcolm were morning people, but one or both of them was clearly eager to talk to Culver, because it was only a little past eight o'clock.

I opened my door, prepared to give a lecture about showing up too early, but the words froze on my lips.

It was Robert standing on my doorstep, and he looked murderous. "Stop interfering with my work," he said, grinding out the words.

My sense of danger turned to one of confusion. "What work?"

"Sam Hart is the reason I'm in Nightmare. He's mine."

CHAPTER SIXTEEN

Robert continued to glare at me while I blinked at him stupidly, partly because I was still trying to wake up, and partly because I had absolutely no idea what he was talking about. I raised a finger. "First of all, I don't even know who that person is." I raised a second finger. "Second, what do you mean, he's yours?"

"You expect me to believe you don't know who Sam Hart is?" Robert looked even angrier now. "Stop pretending you don't know. You and your friends are after the same person I am."

I sighed. "I don't know of anyone by that name. You're going to have to be more specific."

When Robert spoke again, he enunciated the words clearly, like he was addressing a child trying to grasp a difficult concept. "The man who tried to run down Culver in the van. The one you called the police on."

I shut my eyes briefly, trying not to let my own anger rise to the level of Robert's. "You're telling me you've known all along who the man in the van is? And you didn't share that, even after he nearly killed me?"

Robert shrugged. "I didn't know if I could trust you. I still don't. But I need you to get out of my way and stop involving the police, so I can find Hart and capture him. I'm almost certain he's the one who made those ghouls."

"So, he is the resurrectionist, then," I said. That meant our theory about the van turning a lap through the motel parking lot at the same time the witches had done their locator spell was correct. "What's his problem with Culver?"

Robert shrugged. "No idea. I've heard a bit about him and Lakehall, but I don't know what their connection to Hart is."

"Are you going after Culver, too?" And, I wondered, had Robert killed Vincent Lakehall? After all, Robert was a hunter, and Vincent had been a magician.

"Hart is the one with a bounty on him. I can make good money if I bring him in. Culver wouldn't be worth the effort."

"You lied to me," I pointed out. "You claimed you didn't even know ghouls were in Nightmare. You also said you were just here for a nice, relaxing visit with Jeff."

Robert made an impatient noise. "I'm a hunter. We're not in the habit of sharing details about our work, especially not with people who are part of the supernatural community."

Robert had finally come clean with me, so I decided to do the same, as well. I wasn't about to spill my guts to him, but I expected he and I could come to a compromise. "We aren't after this Sam Hart," I told him. "What we are after is someone from the Sanctuary who's missing."

"The owner." Robert nodded. "Shackleford. Jeff told me."

"Baxter is a good man, and he's been missing for a year. We expect the ghouls in the area may be related to his disappearance. If the ghouls are guarding something, it might be Baxter himself. We don't care about Sam Hart, so long as he stops trying to run me over. We just want to get Baxter back."

Robert narrowed his eyes at me. "Then you need to quit calling the police on my target."

That was a promise I couldn't make. I had held information back from Reyes in the past because I had thought it wasn't anything relevant to a murder case he was working, and he had given me a bit of a lecture about it. These days, I was prone to giving him too much information rather than not enough.

Except, of course, any time that information involved the supernatural and things Reyes didn't even know existed in the world.

A sudden thought struck me, and I tilted my head at Robert. "You're the one who killed the ghoul out on the trail."

Robert gave a short laugh. "Actually, I'm not. I don't know who's responsible for that. It could have been Culver or Lakehall."

I trusted Robert about as far as I could throw a gargoyle, but in this instance, I believed him. As a hunter, I figured he would have proudly owned up to killing a ghoul.

"We'll try to stay out of your hair," I told Robert. I meant it, too; none of my friends at the Sanctuary wanted to get in the way of a hunter.

"I appreciate it," Robert said stiffly. He turned and walked down my stairs without another word.

And, of course, the instant he was out of my sight, I shut my door and called Reyes to let him know the van man was named Sam Hart. "I don't know if that helps or not, but I wanted to pass it along," I told Reyes. I hesitated, then added, "Please, don't tell anyone you got this information from me. I don't want to have a target on my back."

"Any more than you already do?" Reyes asked. "Remember, you nearly got killed by this man. You and your friends need to be careful."

Except, it wasn't Sam Hart I was worried about at the

moment, but Robert. Still, I didn't want to tell Reyes, because then he might go have a chat with Robert, and that would only exacerbate things.

Trying to keep the peace—and the secrecy—between humans, hunters, and the supernatural world was not easy sometimes. The gravity of the situation was weighing on me, so in an effort to lighten the mood, I said in a teasing tone, "Are you worried about Justine?"

Reyes was very serious when he answered, "I'm worried about all of you. We've had two stabbings at the state park. I think we have to consider there could be a serial killer in Nightmare."

I wished I could assure Reyes he wasn't dealing with a serial killer, but instead, I made a bunch of promises about taking precautions and keeping an extra eye on Justine.

I had answered the door in my pajamas, so after I got off the phone with Reyes, I got ready for the day. I probably could have used a little more sleep, but my brain was running along at full steam, so there was no point in going back to bed.

I had just finished doing my makeup when there was another knock on my door. This time, I asked who it was before opening it, and Malcolm's voice answered, "Your security detail."

I opened the door to see both Malcolm and Damien standing there, and I waved them inside. "I'll pour coffee while I fill you in on my morning," I said, already heading for the coffee maker.

"I need it," Damien said as he sat down on the small loveseat near the door. Malcolm put his black top hat down on the table and sat on one of the chairs there. "It is entirely too early to be awake after our long night, but I'm ready to get some answers."

"I agree, but in this case, getting up early has been

worth it. I got a key piece of information this morning." I filled Damien and Malcolm in on my visit from Robert.

"Sam Hart," Malcolm repeated when I was finished. "I haven't heard the name, but then, I've never been a part of the larger supernatural scene, especially when it comes to the darker arts."

"Maybe there's no reason to talk to Culver at all," I said. "It seems this Sam guy is our resurrectionist, which means he's the one who can tell us what the ghouls are guarding and where to find it, if we can convince him to talk."

"That means the man we saw on the trail the night of the second murder was not the resurrectionist," Damien mused. "We also know he wasn't Culver or Lakehall."

"The man didn't try to hinder us, so I'm guessing he's not helping guard whatever is out there," I said. "He might be another person searching for it, so he can take it for himself."

"We know the Night Runners are the faction that took Baxter," Malcolm said, "and if Damien's hunch is right that Baxter is mixed up in all this, then maybe they're the ones who have need of ghoul security guards. We have to find out what it is they're guarding. I want to know for sure whether or not Baxter is involved."

"I really do believe he is, and we need to learn as much as we can about what's going on. I still think we need to talk to Culver," Damien said. "Maybe, if we tell him who tried to kill him, he'll give us some useful information in exchange."

It was worth a shot, so after fortifying ourselves with coffee, we took off across the parking lot to the northern wing of the motel.

I knocked on three doors before I got the right room. Thankfully, I hadn't seemed to wake up any of the folks staying in the first two rooms, since they had answered their doors fully dressed—and fully awake.

When Culver answered his door, however, he did look half asleep as he eyed the three of us warily. "What now?" he asked.

"We ran into your van-driving friend in the parking lot last night," Damien said. "Early this morning, really."

Culver's eyes snapped to full attention. "Again?"

"He was apparently doing laps," I told him.

"And why were you in the parking lot in the middle of the night?"

"Oh, you know," I said, "we had just wrapped up an evening stroll with a ghoul."

"Who was made," Malcolm added, "by the very man who tried to kill you. What can you tell us about Sam Hart?"

Culver ran a hand over his face. "That's who tried to run me down? I've heard of Hart. He's ruthless."

"Tell us something we don't know," I intoned.

"Vincent and I came to Nightmare after we heard there was something valuable hidden here," Culver said. "Like the others who have been coming, looking for the same thing. Hart must be determined not to let anyone get their hands on it."

"We've heard the theory about the ghouls guarding something supernatural," I said.

"Some people claim the ghouls are guarding a phoenix." Culver looked at all three of us, clearly savoring our rapt attention. "But that's not all. Word is there's an entire supernatural treasure trove out there."

CHAPTER SEVENTEEN

"What, like a buried treasure?" I asked.

Malcolm gave me a sidelong glance. "Theo is the pirate, Olivia. Not Hart."

"Lucille told us that what we seek is underneath, so that makes me think of buried treasure," I said, undeterred.

Malcolm gave me a searching look. "Lucille? She communicated with you?"

"No, but—we'll fill you in later. In the meantime, Mr. Culver, what can you tell us about this treasure trove?"

Culver spread his hands. "I just told you everything I know. The Night Runners are believed to be the ones keeping things out here, and there's supposedly a phoenix in the mix."

Damien, Malcolm, and I all exchanged a brief look. Our theory that it was the Night Runners behind all this was, apparently, correct. Talking to Culver had been the right move, just as Damien had speculated.

"The night your friend Vincent was killed," I said, "we saw someone else on the trails. You told us enough that we know it wasn't Vincent we saw, but do you know who the man could have been? He might be the one responsible for Vincent's death, but he might also have information about where to find this treasure."

"Did he have dark-brown hair and wild-looking eyes? Long legs and kind of a bouncy walk?"

Damien, Malcolm, and I all nodded.

"I ran into him at the saloon the other night. That's Denny Abel, from the Grim Horizons."

"Grim Horizons?" I asked. It sounded like the name of a rock band.

"Another black-market faction," Malcolm supplied.

Culver nodded. "Exactly."

"That means magicians and black-market factions are converging on Nightmare in a race to find my"—Damien stopped and cleared his throat—"a phoenix."

"Frankly, I'm surprised there aren't more people here looking for it." Culver, thankfully, didn't seem to realize what Damien had almost said. "Or, perhaps, they're doing a better job of laying low than I am."

"We have no interest in the treasure," Damien said. "Just in case you thought we might be competition. We just want to deal with the ghoul problem."

Damien doesn't want Culver or anyone else to come after us, I realized. *And he doesn't want anyone to know that we're after the phoenix, too.*

"Everyone knows you Sanctuary people keep to yourselves and don't deal on the Dire Market," Culver said. "I'm not worried."

We thanked Culver for his help and headed back in the direction of my apartment. "It's early," I said. "I can make breakfast for you two, if you like."

"I'm way ahead of you," Damien assured me. "I picked up a box of cinnamon rolls on my way over here."

"Mama's favorite," I said.

"I know. That's why I got them." Damien gave me a tight smile. "I think she needs to know everything that's happening, since it involves one of her guests, you, and her parking lot. We can have breakfast and fill her in."

Damien retrieved the cinnamon rolls from his car, then the three of us walked up to the office. A guest was checking out when we entered, so we settled into the chairs to wait.

As soon as the guest had walked out, Mama practically pounced on us. "You had another run-in with that van last night."

I looked at Damien, my eyes wide.

"Don't look at me!" Damien said, raising his hands. "I didn't tell her."

Mama crossed her arms. "Hmph. No one had to tell me. I knew."

"You're more psychic than you let on," I told her.

"I saw the van while reviewing security camera footage this morning," Mama admitted. "And, since another van had pulled into the lot around the same time, I just figured something was afoot, and I somehow knew all of you were in the middle of it."

I laughed. "You're absolutely right. But there were a lot of us, and only one of him, so we weren't in any real danger."

"Good." Mama dropped her arms and reached toward the box in Damien's hands. "Besides, I see you brought cinnamon rolls, so I can't be angry."

Mama sat down with us, and we filled her in on the latest news in between bites. Like us, she was cautiously optimistic that when we finally found the alleged treasure trove, we would also find Baxter.

"But you're not going to find him if someone gets to him first," she cautioned. "It sounds like you're racing against all these people who have been descending on Nightmare."

"And not only do we not want to lose Baxter, but we don't want any of those folks to have a phoenix in their possession." Malcolm paused to dust some crumbs off his black coat. "If, in fact, the stash of magical items hidden out there at the state park does belong to the Night Runners, I'm sure they won't let Baxter go without a fight."

"Maybe the fight has already started," I said. "It could be why Sam tried to kill Culver and why he—or someone else—already killed Vincent."

"I've been wondering about that," Mama said. "If Sam wants Culver dead, what's stopping him from just marching up to his door and killing him?"

"Culver is a magician," Malcolm said.

"Why does that make a difference?" I asked.

"It means his room is probably warded with magic." Malcolm waved toward me. "Who knows what might have happened if you had tried to walk across his threshold this morning?"

"You could have forewarned me."

"If you had tried to go into his room, I would have stopped you." Malcolm took another bite of his cinnamon roll, clearly unconcerned. After he swallowed, he said, "By the way, you said you'd tell me about Lucille aiding in our search."

Before I could open my mouth to answer, Mama said, "She's communicating with Lucy. Lucille told her that what we seek is underneath."

Malcolm's lips twitched, and he leaned toward Mama and took her hand. "I'm glad your sister's presence is growing stronger," he said quietly.

"Me, too." Mama squeezed Malcolm's hand, then sniffed loudly. "But before we go getting too sentimental, we have bigger things to think about. I don't like knowing we've got ghouls, a magician, a resurrectionist, and a hunter all lurking around, and Cowboy's Corral is right in the middle of it. Olivia, I don't think you should be on your own at night. You need to stay where you'll be safe."

I blushed and glanced from Mama to Damien. "Oh. Well, I guess…"

Mama suddenly laughed. "I'm not telling you to move in with Damien. I'm saying you should go stay at the Sanctuary until all this blows over."

"Oh! That's probably not a bad idea."

"It's a great idea," Damien said. "But, Mama, you have to agree that you won't be on your own, either. I don't like thinking of you sitting up here by yourself all day, when, like you said, Cowboy's Corral is right in the middle of this mess."

The bell above the door sounded, and we all looked over to see Mama's husband, Benny, coming through the door.

"Perfect timing," Mama said under her breath.

"Two rooms done!" Benny announced with a wide smile. "And good morning, you three. It's been a while."

We all wished Benny a good morning, and he ran his fingers through his gray hair. "It's a good morning, but a busy one. I'm doing paint touchups in all the rooms. The upkeep never ends. Susie, hand me one of those cinnamon rolls before I head over to the next room on the list."

Mama passed Benny one of the pastries, and then he was gone.

"I hope I have that much energy when I'm his age," Damien said.

"His age?" Malcolm said with a sniff. "But he's so young."

"Compared to you, maybe," Mama said. "But there's your answer, Damien. I made a to-do list that will make sure Benny's nearby instead of running errands elsewhere. He'll keep me safe."

"Does he know?" I asked. "About the supernatural world, I mean."

"Baxter trusted him enough to tell him some things,

but Benny has always been a bit of a skeptic. He still thinks the vampires are just regular people who have sleep disorders."

We all got a laugh out of that, and by the time we had finished our breakfast, I was feeling better. Mama had Benny to watch over her, and I would have all my friends at the Sanctuary to do the same for me.

I left Malcolm and Damien to visit with Mama while I went back to my apartment and quickly packed an overnight bag. I had stayed at the Sanctuary before, and I knew there were plenty of guest rooms. And, despite the fact they had once been hospital rooms, they had been transformed into bright, cozy spaces.

Once I was packed, Damien drove me to the Sanctuary, but Malcolm stayed behind. He said it was so he could catch up with Mama, since they had been friends many years before, when Lucille had still been in human form. Since Baxter had cut ties with Mama and Benny in an effort to keep them safe from supernatural threats, that meant everyone at the Sanctuary had also been forced to cut those ties. While I knew Malcolm and Mama were enjoying reconnecting, I also suspected Malcolm wanted to keep an eye on her.

When Damien and I arrived at the Sanctuary, I was struck by how quiet it was. I knew someone was on security duty—either Zach or whomever he had recruited to help —but there was no sign of life. Most of the Sanctuary was asleep.

I didn't want to risk waking anyone up, so I stashed my overnight bag in Damien's office rather than heading upstairs to settle into a guest room. I put my bag down beside the fireplace, then looked at Damien. "What now?"

Damien gave me a sly look. "I've been thinking. That piece of land Emmett is trying to sell is right next to the state park. I think we should go take a look at it."

CHAPTER EIGHTEEN

I grinned at Damien. "Perfect. It's a nice day for being out in the fresh air, too."

Damien and I only made it as far as the entryway before we realized not everyone at the Sanctuary was asleep. Justine was coming down the stairs, muttering under her breath. I saw why when she reached the ground floor. Felipe was right behind her, nipping at her heels.

"Good morning," I said, though it came out like more of a question.

"It would be, if this little monster wasn't driving me up the wall." Justine pointed toward Damien's feet. "Go nibble on *him*."

Instead, Felipe began to trot in a wide circle around the three of us, yipping every few seconds.

Justine sighed heavily. "We're not letting him go out unsupervised because of the ghouls. We boarded up his doggie door, and he is not taking it well."

"Aw, the poor guy just wants to run off some energy," I said, crouching down and waggling my fingers in Felipe's direction.

"Yes, he does, but most of the staff is asleep and can't take him out. I've got to get started on some work in the cemetery vignette, so I can't take him, either." Justine gave

Damien and me an overly sweet look. "But you two are heading out. Wouldn't you like to take Felipe along?"

"Sure," I said. "Where's his leash?"

"There's one hanging up by the back door. Thank you!" Justine turned and disappeared through the door that led to the haunt. Felipe began to follow, but when I called his name, he stopped, his head pivoting between the doorway and me.

Damien patted his thigh. "Come on, boy!" Felipe and I both followed Damien to the back door. Sure enough, the doggie door had been sealed off with a small square of plywood. But, next to the door, there was a purple leash hanging from a hook, along with a black collar that had a row of rhinestones marching around it.

In short order, we were ready to go, but once again, we only got as far as the entryway before we ran into someone else. This time, it was Zach. He was coming in through the front doors, and he seemed startled to see us. "I thought Justine and I were the only ones awake," he said. His eyes flicked down to Felipe. "I'm glad to see you two are getting him off our hands. Four-legged menace."

"Takes one to know one," I said with a wink.

Zach looked at me humorlessly.

"Too early for jokes?" I asked.

"It's too early for bad jokes," Zach corrected. "I do have some news for you two, though. I talked to Laura earlier, and she said a ghoul showed up at the stunt show around six o'clock this morning. She had gone there early because she couldn't sleep, and she figured she'd take a sunrise ride on one of the horses. Instead, she spotted a ghoul."

"First, a ghoul showed up here, and then, one went all the way to the stunt show," I said. "Why are they wandering so far away from this treasure they're allegedly guarding?"

"Treasure?" Zach looked confused.

"According to Jeff's hunter friend, ghouls are often used as guards," I said. "And Culver told us there's supposed to be some kind of supernatural stash out there at the state park."

Zach raised an eyebrow at me. "You two have had as wild of a morning as Laura, it sounds like. Anyway, she kept her distance, and eventually, the ghoul turned around and wandered away."

"At least it didn't cause any trouble," Damien said.

"I wish we knew what was going on. Now, I'm worried about her safety as well as the safety of everyone here." Zach leaned down to gently remove Felipe's jaws from their grip around his left ankle. "That's not all, either. Last night, Laura was unsaddling the horses after the evening stunt show, and she thought she saw someone standing in a corner of the barn. When she tried to look closer, there was no one there, but she was a little shaken by it."

"I'm jumping at shadows, too," I said. "But I do understand why you're worried about her safety. It's bad enough we had a ghoul show up here."

Felipe pointed his snout in the direction of the double front doors and whimpered impatiently.

"He says it's time to go." Damien gestured toward Zach. "You've got others to help with security here. If you want to go keep watch on Laura, that's fine."

Zach's shoulders relaxed. "That place will be crawling with tourists during the daylight hours. She's safe enough. For now."

Those final words felt ominous, and they echoed in my mind as Damien and I finally got out of the building and into his car without any further interruptions. It didn't take long for us to reach Emmett's real estate office, but Damien cruised right past it.

"There was plenty of parking back there," I pointed out.

"Do you want to take an antsy chupacabra into Emmett's office? I figured we would park a few blocks away and let Felipe run off some steam on the walk back to Emmett's."

"Good idea."

Felipe seemed content to finally be out and about after we had parked and were making our way toward Emmett's office. I only heard two people comment on our "weird-looking dog."

Emmett was just unlocking his office door as Damien and I walked up. The space inside was dominated by a large desk, and Emmett bustled behind it and sat down as Damien and I followed him inside.

"Good morning, good morning," Emmett said happily. He reached up to adjust his navy-blue tie, which perfectly matched his pinstripe suit. Emmett was one of the best-dressed people in Nightmare, and I was sure he had to travel to one of the bigger cities to find the expensive suits he wore. Nightmare was a great place to get a cowboy shirt but not a nice suit.

"Tell us more about that property you have out by the state park," Damien said. Felipe's snout was inching toward a pile of papers sitting on the floor to one side of Emmett's desk, and Damien gently tugged on the leash to keep him from shredding the pile with his fangs.

Emmett gave the two of us a knowing smile. "It would be a great place for a house," he reminded us.

"So you mentioned," I said.

"The good news is, the property is still available. The bad news is that I can't take you there right now." Emmett sighed, as if showing us around the land had been what he wanted most to do with his Friday morning. "Still, it's easy enough for you to find the place on your own." Quickly,

128

Emmett gave us directions, which would take us right past the parking lot at the state park.

As Damien and I stood, Emmett did the same. "Let me know what you think of the property," he said, reaching out to shake Damien's hand. "And, when you're ready to build on it, I know a great contractor."

I laughed. "Let's not get ahead of ourselves," I told him.

We walked outside right as Damien's phone rang. He answered it with, "Hi, Zach," then passed the lead of Felipe's leash to me while he walked a short distance away to continue the conversation. I knew Damien wasn't trying to get away from me but from the gaggle of tourists walking past us. He didn't want them to overhear anything about murder or ghouls.

I lazily watched the tourists as they crossed the mouth of the alley near Emmett's office and stepped up to the door of The Lusty Lunch Counter.

As they were going in, Robert was coming out. He was wearing a camouflage jacket and dark-green pants, and he had a plastic takeout bag dangling from one hand. He paused on the sidewalk, throwing glances left and right as if he were on the lookout for someone.

Felipe whined and strained against his leash. "It's okay, boy," I said soothingly. *Can he sniff out a hunter?*

I heard Damien ending his call with Zach as he walked up to me, and I turned to ask if everything was okay back at the Sanctuary. Before I could speak, though, Felipe yelped loudly and jumped forward, ripping the leash right out of my fingers.

Felipe loped toward Robert, who hadn't yet realized he was about to be attacked.

"Felipe, no!" I screamed, right as he launched himself into the air.

CHAPTER NINETEEN

Everything after that seemed to happen in slow motion. Felipe's long front legs were stretched toward Robert, who turned and saw the leathery gray animal sailing right toward him. In one smooth motion, Robert dropped his take-out bag and slid one foot backward, so he was in a deep stance. He raised his arms and crossed them, bracing for the impact.

But Felipe never hit Robert. He landed just inches in front of him, yelped again, and dove his snout into the opening of the take-out bag.

Felipe didn't know Robert was a hunter, nor did he care. He had smelled food, and he wanted it.

Damien and I sprinted across the alley and up to Robert, both of us already apologizing as we skidded to a halt.

"We'll buy you food to replace what he wrecked," I said breathlessly.

"He's just hungry. We're so sorry," Damien added.

Robert was staring down at Felipe, who was oblivious to everything but whatever was inside the take-out bag. From the smell of it, he'd gotten himself a cheeseburger.

"Is that what I think it is?" Robert asked. He finally looked up at Damien and me.

Damien looked around quickly to make sure no one

was standing nearby, then nodded. "Chupacabra," he said under his breath.

"I've never seen one before." Robert sounded more fascinated than angry, and I relaxed slightly. "I had no idea they could be tamed."

I gave a short laugh. "Calling Felipe tame is a real stretch. And we really are sorry about your lunch."

Robert gestured toward the bag. "This wasn't my lunch. This was protection in case I run across any ghouls later. I'm going out to do another search for Sam Hart. I've checked every hotel, motel, and campground in town, but I can't find him or his van."

"Maybe he's staying at someone's home. You have a friend here in Nightmare," I pointed out. "Sam might know someone in town, too."

"It's possible. There's no way he'd be far away from his ghouls, which means he has to be here somewhere."

"I've been saying the same thing about the man we saw on the trail the night Vincent was killed." Mama had been right about unsavory characters descending on Nightmare, and it seemed like I was crossing paths with every single one of them.

The unsavory character standing right in front of me had returned his attention to Felipe. Hesitantly, Robert leaned down slightly. "Can I pet him?"

"Of course," I assured him. "He likes to be scratched behind his ears."

Robert tentatively put his fingers behind Felipe's left ear and scratched. Felipe briefly lifted his head from the bag, his eyes closed and his mouth set in a way that almost looked like a smile. "Wow," Robert said, nearly too quiet for me to hear.

In any other situation, Robert probably would have been working out a way to capture Felipe—or worse. As a hunter, I was sure petting a cryptid known for sucking the blood of goats was not something he would normally do.

Damien offered to go inside and get Robert some more food, but Robert waved him off. "There's enough left in the bag, but thanks." Robert picked up the take-out bag while Felipe was distracted by more head scratches, and as he walked away, he glanced back every few steps.

"Robert was wise to get food before searching for Hart," Damien said.

I nodded. "I've got a tin of mints in my purse, but nothing better for fighting ghouls. We should grab a few snacks in case we need to defend ourselves out at that piece of property we're going to look at."

"No offense," Damien said, reaching down to grab Felipe's leash, "but you're not the best at keeping him under control. I'll watch Felipe while you run to the General Store and grab some things. The stinkier, the better."

"Robert got a cheeseburger. That wasn't stinky."

"Robert is also a trained hunter. We need food that will entice the ghouls to eat it, and I understand a strong scent is a good way to make sure that happens."

I nodded. "Okay. I'll be right back."

Damien decided to walk Felipe around the streets behind Emmett's office, where there were few tourists. I, on the other hand, walked one street over to High Noon Boulevard and plunged right into the crowd of sightseers. A place there called the General Store mostly sold T-shirts, hats, and other souvenirs branded with the town's name, but I knew they also had some snacks.

Less than ten minutes later, I was walking out of the store armed with beef jerky, salt and vinegar potato chips, and a snack mix I had always considered pungent. I had also picked up a small, overpriced bag of dog treats called Nightmare Nuggets. I figured Felipe would enjoy those.

133

I found Damien not far from his car. He had run into someone he knew and seemed to be having a pleasant conversation, though the woman was glancing at Felipe every now and then like she thought she might be seeing things.

I held back while they wrapped up their chat, then Damien led the way to his car. "I went to high school with her," Damien said as we walked. "She was filling me in on all the gossip about people from our class. Some things about this town never change."

"Do you ever regret coming back here?" I asked. Damien had left Nightmare right after high school, and he had been reluctant to come back in the wake of Baxter's disappearance. Only some financial struggles for the Sanctuary had gotten him to finally move back to his hometown.

Damien stepped closer to me and wrapped an arm around my shoulders. "I don't have one single regret." He leaned down and kissed the top of my head. "Though, I confess, I would have gladly gone the rest of my life without seeing a ghoul up close."

"Me, too."

Felipe was a lot more calm on the drive to the property. The exercise and the cheeseburger had settled him down. Meanwhile, I felt more nervous the closer we got.

I was opening the package of beef jerky when Damien glanced at me. "Are you having a snack?"

"No. I'm opening some of the food so it's ready to go in case of an emergency. If we run into a ghoul out there, I want to be ready to throw food in its direction and run."

"You're making my car stink."

I reached over and pressed my finger against the button for the window. "Problem solved," I shouted over the noise of the wind rushing into the car.

Emmett hadn't been kidding about the property being right next to the state park. We passed the parking lot where the witches had done both of their locator spells, and about twenty seconds after that, Damien was slowing down to turn onto a narrow dirt lane nearly hidden by a cluster of low, dusty-looking trees. The only reason we knew where to turn was because of the sign announcing two acres for sale.

Damien pulled forward about fifty feet, then stopped. "We're going to have to walk from here."

The dirt road deteriorated in front of us, filled with holes and ruts. There was absolutely no way Damien's Corvette would have been able to pass.

"Let's go see if we can find ourselves some treasure," I said as I climbed out of the car. "And, if it's worth any money, we can buy you a pickup truck so you can drive down roads like this one."

I was wearing sneakers, but I quickly realized I should have been wearing hiking boots. My shoes were soon covered with a layer of dirt, and I nearly turned an ankle three times in the first five minutes of walking.

We walked for a solid fifteen minutes before the road once again smoothed out, and I could finally stop staring at the ground directly in front of me and look around to see where we were. Emmett hadn't been exaggerating about the views. I stopped walking and gazed at the horizon, where tall hills stretched their spiky peaks toward the cloudless sky.

"This really is a nice view," I said appreciatively. The highest elevation was just to our left, and I could easily picture a house with huge windows perched there.

Damien seemed to be thinking the same thing I was, because he said, "It would make a great location for a house."

"What about the mine?" Decades before, Baxter had purchased Sonny's Folly Mine and revamped it as a home. Damien had been living in it for about six months.

"That's my dad's home," Damien said without hesitation. "When we get him back, he can have it. I prefer a place with windows. I didn't grow up in the mine—I didn't even know it existed—so I've never gotten used to living in such a dark space."

"You must have lived there as a baby," I pointed out.

"If I did, I have no memory of it. Besides, I'd much rather wake up in the morning and get this view."

Yet again, I could feel the way my cheeks warmed at the thought of us buying property and building a house on it. Damien and I weren't really interested in Emmett's property, and we certainly weren't at a point in our relationship where we were ready to discuss our future home together. Still, it felt like we were bumping up against the topic, and it left me feeling slightly breathless.

"I'm sure you don't want your view every morning to be a motel parking lot," Damien continued.

"Not for the rest of my life, no. For now, though, that apartment is exactly where I need to be."

"Except for tonight, when you'll be staying at the Sanctuary."

"Right."

We kept walking, and Felipe began to strain against his leash again.

"Endless energy," Damien said with a sigh. "Does he ever sleep?"

"I've seen Felipe sleep, but it's definitely a rare sight. I don't think—" I cut off as we came around a curve, and I spotted a van parked in the middle of the road.

No, not a van. The van. The one that nearly ran me over.

I grabbed Damien's hand, and without needing to

discuss it, we both began to backpedal, moving as quietly as possible. We had found Sam Hart, the resurrectionist.

And, if we had found Sam, then there were probably ghouls nearby.

CHAPTER TWENTY

Damien and I continued walking backward until the van was completely hidden again by the curve in the road. Felipe seemed confused, because he was straining against his leash, wanting to keep moving forward, while Damien and I were moving backward.

With the van out of sight, we finally turned around and moved as quickly as possible. It was easy at first, but once we reached the stretch of dirt road that was full of holes and ruts, I really had to watch my step. I realized the edges of the road were smoother and moved to the shoulder, but then I found myself at the mercy of weeds that had small thorns on them. They grabbed at my jeans, and a few of the thorns made it all the way through to bite at my skin.

"Ow, ow, ow," I was saying in as low of a whisper as I could muster.

Eventually, we were back in the relative safety of Damien's car. He and I both sat there for a moment, me catching my breath and him looking utterly surprised at having run across Sam's van out there on the property Emmett was trying to sell us.

"What now?" I asked once my heart rate had mostly returned to normal. "Do we go back with fistfuls of beef jerky and confront him?"

"No," Damien said. "Why risk it? We know Sam won't tell us anything, and he's probably armed with more than just ghouls. We don't want Reyes investigating a crime scene for our bodies."

"Reyes! We need to call him and tell him we located Sam Hart. Or, at any rate, we found out where he's parking his van. There's no telling where the man himself is right now."

Damien gave me a sidelong glance. "You don't want to call Robert and tell him the news, instead?"

I made a dismissive gesture. "He'll be mad if he finds out I'm still involving the police in this, but I don't care. I trust Reyes, not Robert. Besides, I don't have a phone number for Robert."

Damien held up his cell phone. "At the moment, though, we're not calling either one of them. No signal."

"Maybe it's not such a great place to build a house, after all."

The only choice was to start driving and call Reyes as soon as we had a signal. Damien said he would head for the police station, even though we knew we would get reception long before that.

We were halfway back to Nightmare when I had enough of a signal, and I wasted no time calling Reyes. As soon as he answered, I said quickly, "We found him! Sam Hart! His van is out on the property that's for sale next to the state park. Oh, it's Olivia Kendrick, by the way."

"Property? That land Emmett Kline is selling? I didn't know you and Damien were that serious."

"What? No, we're not. We were… Oh, never mind. The point is, the van is parked way down the dirt road on that piece of land."

"We're on our way right now. Thanks for the tip, Olivia."

Reyes didn't wait for me to respond before he hung up. Damien had been driving quickly, and he slowed slightly now that we had relayed our message to the police.

"I suppose we don't need to go to the station since Reyes is on the way," Damien said. "Let's take Felipe home, then go grab some lunch. I'm starving after our unexpected hike through the middle of nowhere."

My own stomach growled at the suggestion, and I readily agreed.

Damien was just turning onto the main road through Nightmare when a police car whizzed past us. I didn't catch a glimpse of the officers inside, but I knew Reyes was one of them. "Good luck," I said in the direction of the police car.

The Sanctuary was fairly quiet when we got back, which meant a lot of its inhabitants were still asleep. *Lucky them*, I thought. We removed Felipe's leash, and he went bounding off in the direction of the dining room. Damien and I, however, went to Zach's office to fill him in.

While Damien and I had been a bit shaken by the discovery of the van, Zach seemed relieved by the news. "If he's sticking close to the area the ghouls are guarding, then that means he's far away from us," he said. "I feel better knowing he's hiding out so far away from town."

That viewpoint soothed my nerves a bit, but as my mind relaxed, my attention focused more on my stomach. Damien had been right: a cinnamon roll wasn't nearly enough sustenance to go hiking down a rough dirt road. I was so hungry I was even considering breaking open the salt and vinegar chips, which I generally loathed.

Damien and I had a brief debate about where to go for lunch, but I think we both knew there was really only one option. The Lusty would give us our best chance of seeing Robert again. We knew he wouldn't have had any luck tracking down Sam Hart, since we had done that ourselves, but we were both curious to know if he'd run across any ghouls.

Or a phoenix.

There was no sign of Robert when we arrived at the diner, and I felt a mix of both relief and disappointment. But, not having to track down clues meant I could devote my full attention to devouring a cheeseburger and fries. I cleaned my plate, right down to the last crumb. I spared a thought for Felipe, whom I now knew loved The Lusty's cheeseburgers as much as I did.

After we finished eating, Damien ordered us both chocolate milkshakes. "We've earned them," he told me.

I was slurping down the last of my shake when Jeff walked past and disappeared into the kitchen. Damien nudged me and nodded toward the swinging door that Jeff had gone through. "Let's go say hello."

We paid our bill and skirted behind the stainless steel counter so we could follow Jeff. Not surprisingly, we found him in his office off the kitchen. The space had probably been designed as a closet because it barely accommodated a chair and desk. Damien and I squeezed together in the doorway, since there wasn't room for us to go inside.

"We don't know how to get in touch with Robert," Damien began once we had said hello, "so we're hoping you can pass along a message. We found the guy he's been looking for."

I had to bite my tongue to keep from asking Damien what in the world he was doing. I wanted the police, not Robert, to get Hart. But Damien wasn't done yet. "We called the police, too, since we'd like the guy who almost killed Olivia to be caught."

Jeff narrowed his eyes at Damien. "Robert is trying to catch him, so why involve the police?"

"Because we saw Robert earlier, and he wasn't having

any luck finding Hunt. We do what we can to help the police with their investigations, but we thought Robert would appreciate us keeping him updated, too."

Jeff looked like he wanted to retort, but he seemed to think better of it. After a moment, he sighed heavily. "I'm supposed to be retired."

"Believe me, we wish you weren't having to deal with any of this," I said. "We don't like what's happening, either."

Jeff's expression softened, but his look of sympathy was for Damien rather than me. "I know you want your dad back, and I truly hope you find him. But I'll feel a lot better once these ghouls are gone."

"We all will."

After we left, I waited until we were on the sidewalk in front of The Lusty before I asked, "Why did you tell him that we called Reyes? Robert already lectured me about interfering in his search for Hart, so why let Jeff know that we've just interfered again by telling the police where to find the van?"

"Because Robert would have found out one way or another. You know how the gossip is in this town. Everyone knows everyone else's business. Jeff, at least, would have heard about the police looking for a van out by the park, and he would have passed the news along to Robert. This way, Robert knows we're not hiding anything from him."

I nodded slowly. "You'd rather risk his anger than risk him feeling like we haven't been honest with him."

"He's a hunter. All it would take is a single misstep from one of us for him to go back on his promise to Jeff."

I felt a shiver begin to work its way up from my lower back. I thought it was weird to be so cold when it was such a nice day out, then I realized what I was feeling was my phone vibrating in the back pocket of my jeans. I quickly pulled it out and saw it was Reyes calling.

143

"There was no van and no man," Reyes said glumly. "However, we did find signs someone has been camping out there on Emmett's property, and the tire tracks are fresh. He must have left right after you did."

That meant Hart had known we were there. Damien and I had gotten lucky to avoid a confrontation with him or his ghouls.

I thanked Reyes for the update and told him we were just steps from Emmett's office. "Should we let him know he had a trespasser?" I asked.

Reyes said that was a good idea, especially since the trespasser was also a suspect in two murders. So, once I hung up, Damien and I made our way back over to Emmett's office, hoping he would have returned from his appointment already.

Not only was Emmett there, but he was picking at a salad in a plastic container as we walked in. He hastily swept his lunch to one side of his desk, folded his hands, and gave us what I always thought of as a salesman grin. "Well, you're back. What did you think?"

Damien hesitated a moment, then said, "Actually, we wanted to let you know we discovered someone has been camping on that property. We called the police, but they said by the time they got there, the man had cleared out."

Emmett's face fell. "Oh. He didn't do any damage to the land, I hope."

"Not that we know of," I said. "However, the man did nearly run me over a few days ago, and he's—well, let's just say he's dangerous. In case he comes back, we don't want you to go out there and risk running into him."

"I'll steer clear, for now, but I'm not going to sit by and let someone squat on my land. Especially not when it's scaring off potential buyers, like you two." Emmett stopped, and his nose twitched. "What is that smell?"

"Oh, that's me," I said, reaching over to zip my purse

closed. "Sorry. I've got some beef jerky with me. I also have salt and vinegar potato chips. Would you like some?"

Emmett burst out laughing. "It was a good idea, taking smelly foods to the property with you, but it was completely unnecessary. I could have told you there was no chance of running into a ghoul out there."

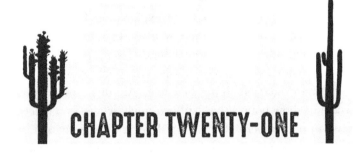

CHAPTER TWENTY-ONE

Emmett began to laugh again as Damien and I stared at him, both our mouths hanging open. Eventually, his laughter softened into a chuckle, and he wiped at one eye. "You seem surprised," he said.

Damien and I looked at each other. I just gave him the tiniest shake of my head, which was my way of asking, *What do we do now?*

"Um, Emmett," Damien began. "I... Did you... I must have misunderstood you. I could have sworn you said 'ghoul.'"

"I did." Emmett smiled, his eyes still dancing with mirth.

Damien started to respond, but after several tries, he finally spread his hands and blew out a breath, too stunned to say anything.

"How do you know?" I asked Emmett.

Emmett waved a hand casually, as if discussing ghouls was a totally normal thing. "I figured it out years ago. Well, I didn't know about ghouls back then, but I realized there was a whole supernatural world. It was my work in real estate that tipped me off."

I laughed nervously. "What, did a vampire ask for a house with no windows?"

I had been making a joke, but Emmett nodded. "I was asked to find a home with a basement that had no windows. The client had some explanation for it, but I found it odd that they insisted on meeting at night, instead of during normal business hours. Then, there was a woman who asked about an indoor pool. Nowhere in Nightmare has something like that. Another time, I was asked to show houses that had extremely secure iron fences around the property. Every time I got a bizarre request, it was for someone who worked at the Sanctuary. Eventually, curiosity got the best of me, and I did a little research."

Damien shook his head. "My father buying a mine and turning it into a home probably raised your suspicions, as well."

"I did find it a bit odd," Emmett admitted, "but at the same time, I thought it was a neat idea. Sonny's Folly Mine was a cheap piece of property, and Baxter saved a lot of money by not purchasing a regular house. By the way, I don't think he ever realized that I know. I certainly never told him."

"Have you ever told anyone?" I asked.

Emmett shook his head with such force his white hair began to fall out of place, and he lifted a hand to push it back off his high forehead. "Of course not. First, who would ever believe me? The people of Nightmare would have thought I was off my rocker. Second, folks at the Sanctuary have always seemed nice enough. There was no reason to expose them."

I raised an eyebrow. "When you and I first met, you seemed a bit unsettled when I said I'd gotten a job at the Sanctuary."

"You were going to be working alongside supernatural creatures," Emmett said. "Of course I was a bit unsettled. But, I couldn't tell you that you might run across a vampire or a siren there, so I had to imply that they were just weird folk at the haunted house. Clearly, you learned their secret pretty early on."

"Seeing someone transform into a werewolf is a quick way to learn," I said. I had been spying on Zach when he had turned, and it would always be one of the scariest, most surreal moments of my life. "This all explains why you realized you had a ghoul on your property, at least."

"I saw him wandering around when I was out there to take some sunset photos for the online listing. I knew he wasn't just a regular human, and it took a bit of digging to figure out he was a ghoul. I went back out there and tracked him down on one of the state park trails. I threw a rare porterhouse steak at him, then left. That was the last time I saw the ghoul, so I guess he ate the steak."

Emmett sighed, and his eyes got a faraway look. "It was a nice cut, too. Just the right amount of fat, and it smelled so good. But, it was worth missing out on eating it myself to get rid of the ghoul. Dead people wandering around hurts sales, you know."

"I can imagine," Damien said. "However, you should know there are more ghouls. And as far as we know, the man who was camping on your property is the resurrectionist who made them."

"No wonder you told me to keep my distance. Rest assured, I'll steer clear, and I won't send any potential clients out there until you two and your Sanctuary friends have this all sorted out. But, please hurry. It's a lot harder to sell land in the summertime, when it's so hot. Now is the perfect season to convince people they need a nice patch of land in the high desert."

"We'll do our best," I promised.

"By the way," Damien said, "since you know my father is supernatural, do you know anything about his disappearance? We've learned he was taken by one of the factions who work the supernatural black market, but if you saw anything, or heard a rumor about his disappearance, it could help us piece together what happened."

"If I had known anything, I would have shared it a year ago, when Baxter first went missing. I do hope he's found safe, and that he's home before too much time passes."

"Me, too. Thank you, Emmett."

I echoed Damien's thanks, and we were turning to leave when Emmett said, "Oh, by the way, did you really think I'd believe that Felipe is a dog?"

"Most people buy it," I said with a lopsided smile.

"I'm not most people."

My smile turned into a grin. "No, you're definitely not."

After Damien and I left, neither one of us spoke until we were in his car and nearly back to the Sanctuary. Both of us, I knew, were thinking over Emmett's bombshell.

It was Damien who finally broke the silence, not by talking but by laughing softly. "Emmett killed a ghoul. Who would have thought?"

"And he's been keeping the Sanctuary's secret for years. I've always liked Emmett, but I have even more respect for him now."

Damien had some work to take care of at the Sanctuary, and it wasn't until we had pulled into the staff parking lot—really just a patch of dirt to the left of the former hospital building—that he said, "Oh, I should have taken you home first."

"No, I'm living here now, remember? At least I am for the moment. Besides, Emmett learning all about the supernatural on his own got me thinking that I should be doing some research of my own, too. All I know about ghouls and magicians is the little all of you have told me. I want to learn as much as I can before we tackle whatever comes next."

With that in mind, I soon found myself in the Sanctuary's library. I hadn't even known it existed until recently, and it had quickly become one of my favorite places in the building. There was one big picture window that looked out over the wild area on one side of the building, but it had thick, dark-red curtains that completely blocked the daylight from coming in when they were closed. I figured that was in case a vampire wanted to read before sunset. I preferred to open the curtains and let the sunshine stream in, making the worn floral carpet look just a bit brighter.

The bookshelves were built-ins, and they stretched all the way to the ceiling. There was a ladder on wheels for reaching the higher shelves, but the first time I had been in the library, I had declared that whatever I read would have to be in arm's reach. There was no way I was going to scramble up that rickety ladder.

I perused the books for a while before finding one titled *The Undead Encyclopedia*. It seemed like a good place to start, so I pulled it off the shelf, brushed a layer of dust off the top of the pages, and settled into a midnight-blue velvet chair.

Once I had read what that book had to say about ghouls, I struggled to get up, because I seemed to have sunk farther into the chair as every minute passed. Eventually, though, I levered myself onto my feet and found another book with the ominous title of *Raising the Dead*.

No sooner had I cracked it open than I heard light but rapid footsteps in the hallway just outside the library, and Clara came running in. "Damien sent me to come get you," she said.

"Is everything okay?" I was instantly worried, and I jumped to my feet. Well, I tried to, at any rate. That squashy chair just didn't want to let me go, and instead of standing, I sort of wobbled my way to the edge of the cushion.

"Everything is fine," Clara assured me as she reached out a hand to help me up. "Sorry if I startled you. I'm excited because Mama and Lucy are here, and our little psychic might have a clue for us!"

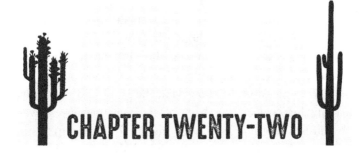

CHAPTER TWENTY-TWO

I put my book about what I assumed was a how-to guide for resurrectionists on a side table, then quickly followed Clara out the door. I hounded her for details as we made our way to the dining room, where she said Mama and Lucy were waiting, but she didn't know any more than she had just told me.

Any shred of worry I was still feeling disappeared when we reached the dining room, and I found Lucy sitting on the floor, giggling as Felipe licked her face. Mama was sitting on one of the benches next to Damien, and Malcolm was standing nearby, pacing slowly.

"Lucy had some news to share as soon as she got to the motel after school today," Mama said. "I told Benny to mind the front desk for a while, and we hot-footed it over here."

I glanced at my watch. School had only been out for thirty minutes, which meant Mama hadn't wasted any time in bringing Lucy to us.

Lucy looked up at me. "Hey, Miss Olivia. I'm here to tell you I saw the ghost on the playground again!"

"That's great news!" I said. Whether or not the ghost was one of the Vanishing Girls, as we suspected, it was still a good opportunity for Lucy to work on her psychic medium skills. "What happened this time?"

"She looked sort of upset. Before, she's looked sad or angry, but today she looked like my friend Callie does when her mom forgets to put chocolate pudding in her lunch. And I said, 'Hey, ghost, what's wrong?' But instead of giving me a normal answer, she said something really weird."

I was so anxious to know what the ghost had said I was leaning forward on the balls of my feet, because it was obviously something important enough for Mama to hustle Lucy to the Sanctuary. Lucy didn't show any signs of continuing, though, so I prompted, "What did she say?"

"'Hidden underneath.'" Lucy rolled her eyes. "Like I said, weird. I don't know how this ghost thinks I'm going to be able to help if she won't tell me what she needs."

I looked up at Damien. "Déjà vu," I said.

"Yes," Malcolm said, "another reference to something being underneath."

"Just like Lucille said to Lucy," Damien added.

"No," I said slowly. "I mean, yes, but that's not the memory I'm thinking of. Remember the tarot reader at the Nightmare Arts Festival last month? When I got my cards read, she laid out three cards, but the one that represented my future had another card stuck to the back of it. The Prisoner."

Damien's back straightened as he sucked in his breath. "That's right. She told you its placement represented something hidden underneath."

"Exactly. I took it literally, because Baxter is a prisoner, and he's hidden from us. The reader had a metaphorical explanation for that extra card, but I think my hunch was right. The concept of something being hidden showed up in my cards, Lucille said it, and, now, the ghost at the playground has said it."

"But, unfortunately, it still doesn't help us find my

father." Damien seemed to shrink again. "Besides, that would imply a connection between him and the ghost girl Lucy sees."

"Malcolm," I said, "are ghosts valuable? I mean, could someone use them for doing magic, or something?"

"Sure. Ghosts have all kinds of uses. You've utilized Tanner and McCrory to check out locked places you couldn't get into yourself."

"What if the ghosts of the three Vanishing Girls are part of this alleged treasure trove the ghouls are guarding? Maybe the ghost Lucy sees can escape sometimes, just long enough to show up on the playground at school for a few seconds."

"And she's trying to point us toward where she and the others are hidden," Damien said.

I nodded. "It would explain why the ghost has looked both angry and sad in the past. She's trapped. That means the treasure trove has been there for decades, but we're only now learning about it. We thought Lucille was being cryptic when she told Lucy that what we sought was hidden underneath, but she was being literal. The treasure the ghouls are guarding is hidden somewhere underneath the trail system!"

"What's a ghoul?" Lucy asked. I looked down to see her gazing at me with a tilted head.

"It's sort of like a ghost," Mama said quickly.

"Oh. Okay." Lucy went back to playing with Felipe.

Thank you, I mouthed to Mama. I had gotten so excited I had forgotten about the young ears listening to our conversation.

"You know," I said thoughtfully, "when Jared Barker was killed, it was for a small mine located on his ranch. Emmett told me at the time that there are dozens of little mines in the vicinity. Baxter, the Vanishing Girls, and whatever else is part of that supernatural hoard could be in an old mine, or even a cave."

"By the way," Damien interjected, "Emmett knows about us."

"Damien, honey, everyone knows you two are dating," Mama said. "You two are hot Nightmare gossip."

"No," Damien said, giving Mama a significant look. "He *knows*. So many people at the Sanctuary have made bizarre real estate requests over the years that he finally caught on."

Mama snorted out a laugh. "Clever man!"

"I think it's time to ask the witches to join our discussion," Malcolm said, quietly enough that Lucy wouldn't hear him. "I expect we'll need their magic before this is all said and done." He was already walking toward the door before he finished talking.

There was a lot I wanted to say, but I reminded myself not to spill the beans to Lucy. When Malcolm returned a few minutes later with Morgan, Madge, and Maida trailing in his wake, Mama quickly suggested Maida and Lucy take Felipe out for a walk. The two girls instantly agreed, and as soon as they were gone, we told Morgan and Madge our theory.

I felt a bit justified for having referred to the supernatural stash as a buried treasure.

"No wonder the locator spell to find Baxter failed," Morgan said with a chuckle. "We should have been using a map of Nightmare, like we did when we were trying to pin down the resurrectionist."

Madge had a thoughtful look on her face. "Perhaps our spell did work, but we didn't realize it. When the snake slithered right off the picnic table, we thought it was because it couldn't find a location for Baxter on the maps of Georgia. But, perhaps, it fell on the ground because Baxter is somewhere underneath that very area."

"Can you try again?" Damien asked.

"Yes, but be warned that it's likely to fail or give us confusing results," Morgan said. "The ghouls won't be the only thing guarding the treasure. That cache will be heavily warded with cloaking magic."

"But it's worth a shot," Madge added.

We decided we would wait until after work that night to try the locator spell. That ensured no one would see the witches at work and wonder what they were up to. They had done the first spell in broad daylight, but one time was simply unusual. Any more than that, and people would really begin to wonder what was going on. The witches would become hot gossip in Nightmare, just like Damien and me.

Of course, if we ran into yet another random night-time hiker, the witches would have a witness to their spell work. I didn't like knowing the guy—Denny, I remembered Culver had called him—was still wandering around Nightmare. Finding Baxter was our goal, but knowing Denny and Sam Hart and even Robert were on their way to some other town would be a nice prize, too.

I was preparing to head back to the library when Zach and Laura both came in. She didn't look worried, and when I asked her how she was doing, she said, "No ghouls have shown up at my work today, so I'm taking that as a win."

"Damien, someone is at the door, and he's asking for you or Olivia," Zach said. Unlike his girlfriend, Zach did look slightly worried.

"Who is it?" Damien asked, sounding wary about having an unannounced visitor.

"None other than Olivia's neighbor Jimmy Culver."

"He can come in here if he wants to talk," Mama said. "He's staying at my motel, and I want to know if he's up to no good."

Zach said he and Laura were heading out the front doors, anyway, so they would direct Culver back to where we were sitting. We didn't have to wait long for Culver to burst through the door, looking shaken.

"I need help," he said, looking around at all of us. When his eyes landed on Mama, he started. "Oh, hello."

"What have you done now, Mr. Culver?" Mama asked. She normally had a friendly, welcoming demeanor, but she had given up pretending to like Culver. I couldn't blame her.

"Abel is after me now, too."

We all stared in confusion at Culver, who clarified, "Denny Abel. The guy I told you is a member of the Grim Horizons."

"Oh, the trail guy!" I said as the name clicked.

Culver looked at me like he wanted to comment, but instead, he gave his head a little shake and turned to Damien. "With Abel and Hart after me, I didn't know where else to go. I came here to beg for protection."

"Why don't you just leave town?" Damien asked.

Culver hesitated, and I knew he wasn't willing to leave Nightmare because he didn't want to give up on the treasure yet, but what he said was, "They might follow me."

"If we protect you," Damien said, stepping close to Culver, "it will put everyone at the Sanctuary in danger. The last we need is for this Denny Abel and a bunch of ghouls to show up on our doorstep.

"Denny might come, but the ghouls won't," I said. When everyone turned to look at me in surprise, I added, "At least, I don't think they will. We've got a couple of hours before we open the haunt tonight, and I want to test a theory I have."

Damien had been glaring at Culver, but he smiled as he asked me, "And what's your theory?"

"The ghouls aren't just guarding the treasure," I said. "I think they're also tracking down any treasure that escapes. Come on, we're going to the playground at Nightmare Elementary School."

CHAPTER TWENTY-THREE

Malcolm's eyebrows slowly rose. "Ah," he said as his dark eyes lit up. "An excellent theory, Olivia."

"Please, enlighten me," Mama said.

"The ghost Lucy has seen on the playground has been showing up for months now," I explained. "But this week, other ghosts have been spotted, too. I overheard Fiona mention seeing a ghost here at the Sanctuary the same day that ghoul showed up at our door. Then, Zach told us Laura thought she spotted someone in the barn at the stunt show, but when she looked again, no one was there. Early that next morning, a ghoul showed up at the barn, stood around for a while, then left."

"You think ghosts who are part of this supernatural treasure are escaping for brief moments," Mama said, nodding. "And I'm guessing Lucy's spectral friend taught them how to do it."

"It stands to reason, then, that a ghoul has been dispatched to go get the Vanishing Girl on the playground," I continued. "Of course, she's long gone, since she only shows up for a few seconds, but the ghouls are so slow that there's no way one has arrived yet."

"But there was never a report of a ghoul on the playground before, and Lucy has seen the ghost a number of times," Mama pointed out. "Even someone who didn't know about the supernatural world would notice a person with rotten skin shuffling around like a zombie."

"But there haven't been ghouls in Nightmare, until recently," Damien said. He was looking at me proudly. "After the Night Runners realized word was out about their treasure trove, they brought Sam Hart in to make a ghoul security squad."

"And I'm guessing I know how word got out in the first place," I said. I looked at Damien and bared my teeth.

Damien made a noise of disgust. "Orin. That tooth fairy probably realized my father had never been taken out of Nightmare. He came here claiming to help us, and he found something that tipped him off to my father being in our own backyard. He told his people, someone let it slip, and now we're awash in ghouls."

"And unsavory characters," Mama added, looking pointedly at Culver.

"It all makes sense," Culver said, ignoring Mama's comment. "Victor and I first got word of it about three weeks ago. I'm guessing this Orin character was here not too long ago?"

"A couple months ago, yes," Damien said.

"Tooth fairies," Malcolm muttered.

"The Night Runners were smart to amp up the watch," Culver continued. "If they're hiding things that can help them gain more power, then it would be a disaster for them if someone stole or destroyed the stash."

Sam Hart had come to Nightmare to make ghouls that would protect the Night Runners' treasure. Jimmy Culver, Victor Lakehall, and Denny Abel had all followed, hoping to get their hands on those valuable magical items.

And Victor Lakehall had been killed for it.

Did Culver kill him? I wondered. He was still at the top of my suspect list. He hadn't seemed upset about Victor's death when I told him about it, but he might have been so

162

shocked that he hadn't been able to process it in those few seconds before we were almost killed by Hart.

If someone had asked me to conjure in that moment, I'm not sure what I would have done. I desperately wanted to find Baxter, but I was also anxious to know who had killed Victor.

Luckily, no one was asking me to conjure anything, so I again stated that it was time for us to head to the school playground. We had a date with a ghoul.

Mama stood and gave her hair a gentle pat. "I'll take Lucy back to the motel. Ghoul-hunting is not my idea of a fun afternoon."

"What about me?" Culver asked Damien as Mama went off in search of Lucy. "Is there a room I can stay in, or what?"

"Oh, no," Damien said ominously, "you're going with us to the playground. I don't want you out of my sight just yet."

"But—" Culver began, but he cut off abruptly at a look from Malcolm.

We must have made a strange group when we arrived at the playground. Damien had driven Culver there, while Malcolm and I had convinced Justine to take us in her car. Actually, we had asked to borrow her car, but Justine said that wherever her car went, she went.

Really, I knew Justine just wanted to see what would happen, but I couldn't blame her for being curious. Even I was excited to know if my theory was correct.

Malcolm, Culver, and Damien all stood at one edge of the playground, but Justine and I walked over to the swings and each sat down on one. The students were long gone for the day, so we had the playground to ourselves, and she and I slowly swung back and forth as we kept an eye out for a ghoul.

We waited for a long time, and I was just about to give up when Malcolm called softly, "We have company."

I glanced around but saw no one, so I looked at Malcolm. He was staring at the overgrown area behind the swings, his arms and legs bent slightly. He looked like an animal about to pounce on its prey.

I looked in the same direction as Malcolm but didn't see anything among the trees and tall vegetation. After a few moments, though, I did hear the crunch of someone walking over rocks. Justine and I both stood in unison, waiting for the ghoul to appear.

Except, when the person did appear, it wasn't a ghoul at all. For the second time, we had been expecting the walking dead, and what we got instead was a living person. The same living person who had surprised us on the trail the night Victor had been killed.

Denny Abel from the Grim Horizons.

"Are you kidding me?" I said before I could stop myself.

Culver had an even stronger reaction than I did, because he rounded on Damien and roared, "You set me up! You knew he would be here, too!"

Damien had clearly not been expecting the accusation, and he blinked at Culver, too stunned to respond.

Malcolm, however, came to his rescue. "I expect," he said calmly, "he followed us here and finally got tired of waiting for something to happen." Malcolm turned toward Denny. "Hi, there! Are you here to confront Culver?"

Denny had been walking closer, but he stopped and looked from Malcolm to Culver. "Uh, yes, as a matter of fact. I was going to hide back there to see what you were up to, but you don't appear to be doing anything at all."

"I told you," Malcolm said to Culver.

"You killed Victor," Culver shouted, glaring at Denny. "And, now, you're going to kill me, too."

"If I had killed that magician, I would be bragging about it to everyone I met. However, I am not so lucky. I expect you killed him, because the two of you hated each other."

"You lie."

"Do I? I know about Cleveland."

Culver paled, and Denny plowed ahead. "In fact, I understand it was one of my Grim Horizons brothers who intervened to keep you from casting a deathless sleep spell on Victor."

"You also kicked Victor out of the motel room here, because the two of you had such a bad fight," I added.

Culver threw me a look that made me take a step back. "Fine, yes, all of that is true," he spat. "But we knew it would take our combined magic to find the Night Runners' treasure, and we thought we could get along long enough to find it. Obviously, we were wrong. But I didn't kill him! You have to be the one who murdered him, because—"

"Enough!" Malcolm said. He barely raised his voice, but it carried so much weight that both men fell silent. Malcolm then turned to me. "Olivia, I expect the ghoul is still some distance away. Unfortunately, we can't afford to wait any longer."

I glanced at my watch. Malcolm was right. The family meeting would start in less than half an hour, which meant it was time for all of us to get to work.

"Please don't follow us back to the Sanctuary," Damien said to Denny. "We'll be crawling with guests tonight— normal, non-supernatural people who are completely oblivious to all of this. It's not a place to confront Culver, or anyone else."

Not surprisingly, Denny refused to make any such promise. He narrowed his eyes at Damien, muttered something under his breath, then turned and stalked off.

"You see why I came to you for protection?" Culver said as soon as Denny was out of earshot.

"I see why you need looking after," Damien answered. "Malcolm, I want you, Gunnar, and Theo to take turns watching him tonight. Make sure he doesn't do anything stupid."

Culver snorted. "I've done my research on your residents. I'm not afraid of your tame vampire or your gargoyle."

"Are you afraid of me?" Malcolm asked.

"I don't even know what you are."

Malcolm closed the gap between himself and Culver in three strides, leaned down, and whispered something in Culver's ear. When he straightened up, Culver swallowed hard and took a step back.

Apparently, he was afraid of Malcolm, after all.

Justine told me on the drive back to the Sanctuary that I was going to be posted at the front door again that night. I was grateful I could be there to keep an eye out for Denny, Sam, or even Robert, because I had a hunch we were heading right for a massive confrontation. It almost felt like the air around me had a charge to it, giving me a little tingle that made the hair on my arms stand up.

Despite my feeling that we were on the verge of something, the first two hours of door duty that night were the same as they were every Friday: nonstop guests streaming in, lots of questions about where the bathroom was, and a few screams from people who were scared before ever entering the haunt.

During my break, I told Mori how I was feeling. I had expected sympathy, so I was surprised when she said, "I'm so proud of you, Olivia!"

I cocked my head. "What?"

"Being a conjuror puts you in the same supernatural category as people like Justine and Vivian. Your magic comes from your mind. The feeling you're experiencing right now is your mind reading the signs and telling you what's about to happen. Your magic is growing." Mori grinned at me, her fangs looking especially long against her blood-red lips.

"And, maybe, I can conjure some control over whatever is coming," I mused.

"Yes, perhaps."

By the time my break had wrapped up, I was almost feeling excited. Something was going to happen, and when it did, I would be ready for it.

And yet, even with that mentality, I was still startled when Clara came running up to me just moments after I had started taking tickets again.

"I just saw a ghost!" she said, not bothering to lower her voice. Anyone nearby would simply think it was part of the show.

I grinned at Clara. "Good. Time to test my theory again. Now we wait for a ghoul to show up."

CHAPTER TWENTY-FOUR

The ghoul showed up twenty minutes before we closed for the night. I first knew something was amiss when the short line of people still waiting to get inside began to grumble, then they all jostled each other as they shifted to one side.

"Oh, the smell!" a man yelled.

"Are they trying to scare us or make us sick?" a woman chimed in. "It's not funny, and it's not even scary. It's just gross."

I slid past the people whose tickets I was tearing so I could see what was happening under the portico. Zach had also noticed the scene, and the entire top half of his body was leaning out the ticket window.

The ghoul was dressed in filthy green shorts and a long-sleeved T-shirt, and the people had been right: he stank. He must have been dead for a while.

"I think your employee is drunk," a young woman standing at my elbow said. "He can barely walk."

I made a humming noise. "A real shame. We'll get him inside." I looked toward the ticket window to catch Zach's eye, but he had disappeared. A moment later, he stepped up behind me.

"Zach," I said quietly, "it appears this employee is drunk, as this guest has pointed out. Let's help him into the dining room."

Zach wordlessly stepped around me and moved so he was between the ghoul and the people in line. He held his arms out, not touching the ghoul but guiding it straight toward the door. As Zach followed it into the entryway, he whispered, "Damien's office. The entryway is too crowded to safely get to the dining room."

In a few minutes, both Zach and the ghoul had disappeared. By then, everyone in line was babbling, and I caught the word "drunk" several times.

Good. Let them believe that's what happened.

A few minutes later, Malcom sailed past me, going in the direction of Damien's office. That meant the ghoul would be well-guarded, and Zach could return to the ticket window for the last few sales of the night.

As the excitement calmed down, I started doing the math. Clara had seen a ghost less than two hours before, which meant there was no way the ghoul could have made it all the way from the state park in such a short time. Either my theory that the ghouls were being dispatched to collect escaped ghosts was wrong, or the ghoul had gotten a head start.

I had the wild idea that Sam Hart had dropped the ghoul off, letting him out of the van to come and collect the ghost. That, of course, was extremely unlikely. It made a lot more sense this ghoul had gone to collect the ghost Lucy had seen on the playground, but when that attempt had come up empty, it had continued on to catch the ghost spotted at the Sanctuary.

That meant ghouls had a way of knowing when someone—or something—escaped from the treasure hoard. I wondered if they were telepathic or had some other means of communication.

At the moment, though, I had more important things to worry about, like what we were going to do with the ghoul we had in captivity.

As soon as we closed for the night, I practically sprinted to Damien's office. The door was open, and I walked in, ready to be horrified.

Instead, I laughed. Malcolm was relaxing in one of the wingback chairs. The ghoul was staring at the fireplace, motionless. There was no need to worry it was going to get away, because Malcom had somehow secured Felipe's collar around its neck, and Malcolm was holding the other end of the leash in his hand. The rhinestones on the collar glittered, a stark contrast to the ghoul's discolored, decaying skin.

Once I had recovered from my first glimpse of the strange scene, I asked, "What now?"

Damien sighed. "We take it home, then see what happens."

I wrinkled my nose. "What are we going to do, drive it back to the state park?"

"Would you rather spend hours following it while it walks home?"

"Good point. I just never thought we would be some kind of dead-guy chauffeur service."

The only option was to load the ghoul into Fiona's van, because not one of us was willing to put it in the back seat of our cars. It took some work, but eventually, the ghoul was crouched in the back of the van. Malcolm sat as far away as possible, the end of the leash still secure in his hand.

It felt like the entire Sanctuary was a part of our caravan out to the park, with the exception of Mori, Theo, and Seraphina, who all stayed behind to keep watch. We had four vehicles driving in a line, while Gunnar flew over-head, high enough that he wouldn't be spotted by any tourists still lingering on High Noon Boulevard. We even brought Culver with us, because Damien wanted to keep an eye on him.

The witches rode with me, ready to try the locator spell to find Baxter again. Every time I got excited that we might actually recover Baxter within a matter of hours, they would caution me not to get my hopes up. Their magic would likely be up against the magic of the Night Runners.

When we arrived at the state park, I offered to help the witches set up their locator spell while Fiona, Malcolm, and Zach got the ghoul unloaded from the van. Nearby, Damien stood in a tight circle with Clara and Justine. The two of them had heard about the ghoul's arrival shortly before we all headed out the door, and I knew Damien was filling them in on our plan.

The picnic table was soon spread with the necessary items for the locator spell, so I took a moment to open my purse and make sure the beef jerky that was still in there was within easy reach.

The ghoul had immediately started shuffling down one of the trails as soon as it was out of the van, and Malcolm looked like he was walking a ghastly dog as he followed. The witches stayed at the picnic table while the rest of us walked behind Malcolm.

Damien reached out and took my hand. "It's going to work this time," he said quietly.

I squeezed his fingers. "Are you trying to reassure me, or are you reminding yourself? Either way, yes, I'm confident we're getting somewhere." I thought of the feeling I'd had earlier in the night, that sense something big was on the horizon.

"Looks like we've already gotten somewhere," Damien said. He nodded toward the ghoul, which had stopped moving forward. Instead, it began to walk back and forth across the trail.

"Why is it pacing?" I asked.

Even though I had been speaking quietly, Malcolm

heard me and said, "He's not pacing. He's guarding." Malcolm matched the ghoul's steps so he could take off the collar.

"Guarding what? We've been down this trail, and we haven't seen anything that could hold a phoenix, or any other kind of supernatural things."

"The stash is hidden underneath, remember?" Damien reminded me. "The witches will tell us which rock to look under."

We assumed the ghoul would stay put, so we returned to the witches to see if they were having any luck. When we walked up to the picnic table, we were just in time to see Maida cross her arms and stomp her foot.

"Trouble?" Clara asked.

"Triple trouble," Morgan said.

"Bad things always come in threes," Madge agreed.

"Except us. We're good," Maida said in a pouty tone.

Justine laughed softly. "You're going to have to translate for us. What do you mean 'triple trouble'?"

"The locator spell has worked, but it indicated three points on the map," Morgan explained. "It's possible all are decoys, designed to lead us to the wrong place."

Madge brushed a strand of hair out of her face. "But it's also possible one is the real spot, and the other two are traps."

"Which means we have to choose and hope we do not choose the wrong one," Maida concluded.

"Clever," Justine said. "We're going to have to be careful if there are magical traps around here."

After some discussion, we decided to send one group to the first spot on the map the locator snake had indicated while another group would head for the second spot. The witches, meanwhile, agreed to keep an eye on Culver.

Damien and I teamed up with Justine to check out the

second location, which was a bit farther away from the parking lot than the first spot.

"Great, more midnight hiking," I groaned.

"Be on the lookout for more ghouls," Damien warned me.

The trail we had to take to reach the spot got us most of the way there, but when the path made a sharp left-hand turn after around fifteen minutes of walking, we had to keep going straight.

Even the flashlight I kept in my car wasn't nearly bright enough to illuminate all the brambles, thorns, and otherwise pokey parts of plants that attacked me.

"And here I was worried about ghouls," I said as I carefully pulled my leg out of the clutches of a low, thorny tangle of vines. "Desert plants are more dangerous than any supernatural creature I've run across."

"I'd take a ghoul over a cactus any day," Justine agreed. Her long hair had been getting tangled up with so many low-hanging spindly branches that she had pulled it back and tucked it inside her black Nightmare Sanctuary hoodie.

"You just have to step carefully," Damien said as he led the way through the underbrush. "I'm not having any—"

Damien's body seemed to glide forward a couple of feet, and he pinwheeled his arms in an effort to keep his balance. There was a loud crunching sound before he stopped moving.

"Stay where you are!" he called.

Justine and I immediately froze. "Are you okay?" I asked. I could hear the panic in my voice.

"Yes," Damien said, sounding like he wasn't at all sure that he was. "There are a bunch of loose stones here where the ground begins to slope downward. They almost slid me right over the edge of a cliff."

Justine held her flashlight aloft, and I gasped. Damien

really had slid to the edge of a sudden drop-off. If he hadn't been able to stop himself, he would have fallen right over the cliff.

"We're at the location indicated on the map," I pointed out.

Damien was slowly backing up, moving at a snail's pace so he wouldn't become a human landslide again. "We were expecting some kind of magical trap, but this is just as bad," he noted.

"I told you the desert was more dangerous than the supernatural." I waited until Damien had backed up all the way to where Justine and I stood before I let out a relieved sigh. "Let's hope the others aren't being led to something even worse."

With no cell phone signal in the area and no radio in hand, we couldn't call and warn the other group to be extremely mindful of where they stepped. Our only choice was to retrace our steps.

I relaxed as soon as the parking lot came into view again, and I spotted Malcolm talking to Clara. The other group had returned safely.

"What did you find?" Damien called as we came up to them.

"An old mineshaft," Malcolm said. "One of those that's just a narrow hole leading straight down into the ground. If Clara hadn't spotted it, I would have walked right into it."

"That only leaves us with one more location to try," I said. "Maybe the third time is the charm?"

"Unfortunately, no," Fiona said. Her husky voice was quieter than usual. When she was upset, her pitch and volume would rise until she reached full banshee wail. I wasn't sure what it meant when she was so quiet, but if I'd had to guess, I would have said she was frustrated and disappointed. "We didn't have as far of a walk as your group, so we also checked the third location indicated on the map. It was nothing but a pile of rocks crawling with scorpions."

"I have a suggestion," Clara said. She was staring down at the map, and she pressed a finger against it. "Why don't we try the spot right in the middle of the three locations the spell gave us? It's not far from where the ghoul was pacing earlier."

"It's worth a shot," Damien said. "We have no idea where else to search."

"And I'm thinking those three decoy spots were purposely chosen not just for their danger but for their relative location to the real treasure." Clara dragged her index finger in a wide circle that encompassed all three spots. "We've been seeing ghouls in this area, so whatever they're guarding is close to the decoys. At the same time, anyone who identified one of these three decoy spots would think they'd found the real site because of the presence of the ghoul guards."

The spot Clara had pointed out was between two trails, so we chose one and walked along it until we seemed to be in about the right area. Even the witches came along, since they had completed their spell.

We were trying to choose a good place to dive off the trail when Justine said, "We're close. Look."

She was pointing at a trampled area, where someone had been walking. We followed the beaten path in single file, until the space opened up, and we found ourselves standing in a small clearing of sorts.

There was a rocky hill on our right, and, nearly hidden by the way two boulders were sitting, was the entrance to a small cave. Three ghouls stood in front of it.

"Excellent," Malcolm said as I hastily dug some beef jerky out of my purse.

We were quietly discussing a plan when there was the

sound of footsteps behind us. I whirled around, waving a stick of beef jerky in front of me, only to see Robert.

"I expect one of these freaks is your serial killer," Robert said.

There was the sound of more footsteps, and Luis Reyes appeared next to Robert.

CHAPTER TWENTY-FIVE

"They're not freaks," Reyes said sternly. "They're friends."

Robert turned and glared at Reyes. "It's bad enough Jeff likes these people, but you, too?"

"What are you two doing out here?" I asked.

Reyes glanced at me, then his eyes fixed on Justine. "Robert said he thought he knew where we might find Sam Hart. We weren't expecting to run into any of you."

Malcolm snorted and crossed his arms. "I'm pretty sure Robert followed us here."

"Who are those men, and what's wrong with them?" Reyes asked tensely.

Oh, boy. Looks like Nick and Mia won't be the only ones getting The Talk from us about the supernatural.

"Luis," Justine said, her voice quavering slightly, "I promise I'll explain, but first, we have bigger issues." She pointed behind the two men, and they both turned as two ghouls stepped out of the shadows. One of them was the ghoul we had brought with us from the Sanctuary.

Reyes's hand strayed to his gun holster, but in one smooth motion, Robert pulled out a fast-food cheeseburger, unwrapped it, and handed it to the ghoul. The ghoul eagerly, albeit slowly, took a bite, swallowed, then collapsed to the ground, motionless.

"What did you do?" Reyes nearly shouted, his head whipping around to stare at Robert.

"I gave him a cheeseburger," Robert answered calmly.

"You just killed that man."

"No, I didn't."

"But I just saw——"

"He's right," I cut in. I suddenly felt like my heart was beating at twice its normal pace. "Robert didn't kill that man. But he did kill Victor Lakehall."

Now it was my turn to be stared at as both Reyes and Robert swiveled toward me.

"Sam Hart obviously killed Victor," Robert said with a sneer. He jerked his chin in Culver's direction. "Now, he's after Victor's business partner."

"You knew you weren't going to find Sam Hart out here tonight," I countered. "Damien told Jeff that Hart had taken off from Emmett's property next to the state park, and he passed that tip on to you. There's no way Hart would come back to this area. It would be too risky for him."

Robert glared at me, but I felt Damien standing next to me, and I knew the rest of my friends were nearby. I had nothing to be afraid of. "You didn't come here to find Hart," I continued. "You're here to find the same thing as us. After you realized we were coming here, you called Reyes in the hopes he would run us off, and you'd be able to keep whatever is inside for yourself."

"Inside what?" Reyes asked. "That little cave behind you?

"Yes," I said. I glanced back and saw the three ghouls guarding the entrance had stepped closer to us. "Robert heard the same rumors as everyone else about there being valuable things hidden out here. We've been focusing on people who would want to possess those things, but Culver also said someone might destroy them. I didn't think

anything of it at the time, but seeing you here, I remembered that. You've been claiming you're in town to track
down Sam Hart, but you really want what he came here to
help guard."

Robert opened his mouth to protest, but Reyes held up
a hand to silence him. "Let her talk," he commanded.

"When you couldn't find the treasure yourself, you told
us the ghouls were guarding something. You already knew
we're looking for Baxter, so you assumed we'd take up the
search here, and we'd lead you right to the treasure." I
shook my head and grimaced. We had played right into
Robert's hands. "That's exactly what we did tonight. You
want to destroy everything inside the cave, including
Baxter."

"Baxter?" Reyes was looking between Robert and me.
"Baxter Shackleford?"

"Yes," Damien said. "My father."

"Again, Luis," Justine said, "I will tell you everything
once we're past all this."

I could hear the strain in Justine's voice, and my heart
broke for her. This wasn't how she had wanted Reyes to
find out about the supernatural world, and there was no
telling how he would take the news.

"You think he'll believe you?" Robert asked, looking at
Justine like he wanted to laugh.

"Yes," Justine answered. There was no trace of doubt
in her voice. She might be afraid of how Reyes would
react, but she knew he would believe her.

Robert shook his head. "He should be arresting all of
you for interfering in a murder investigation."

"But you're the one who committed the murder in the
first place," I said. "You're the one Luis should arrest!"

The other ghoul that had come up behind Reyes and
Robert had been slowly moving closer, and Robert turned
and handed it what looked like an apple slice. The ghoul

put the whole thing in its mouth, then promptly collapsed at Robert's feet.

"The crime," Robert said calmly as he returned his attention to all of us, "is not destroying the abominations inside the cave."

Damien took a step forward, his hands curled into fists. "My father is not an abomination!"

There was a loud scraping sound and a rumble behind me, and I knew a rock had toppled off the hill and landed with a thud on the ground. I leaned forward to get a look at Damien's face, and not surprisingly, his eyes had a green glow to them. He was getting upset, and he had unleashed a wave of psychic energy that had moved the rock.

I reached out and put my hand on Damien's back. *Damien is calm,* I repeated to myself, over and over, in an attempt to prevent him from getting so upset that he put someone in danger.

Robert's anger flared, and he moved toward Damien, looking ready to swing a punch. "Your father is dangerous. Do you know what a magician like him"—Robert stabbed a finger in Culver's direction—"could do with a phoenix? If I hadn't gotten rid of the other one, they would already have their hands on the bird. You should all be calling me a hero."

Robert's body stiffened, and his eyes widened as he realized what he had just said.

"That sounds like a confession to me," Reyes said, pulling a set of handcuffs off his belt. "Robert Pace, you're under arrest for the murder of Victor Lakehall and three other victims whom have yet to be identified."

"He's only guilty of one murder," I clarified. Reyes finished handcuffing Robert, then looked at me quizzically. I waved the beef jerky in the air, then took a bite of it. I gagged as I quickly chewed and swallowed. "Yuck! I really don't like this stuff."

I offered the jerky to Reyes. "Here, take a bite," I instructed.

Reyes looked confused, but he complied. After how strange the night had become, I supposed he was just going with the flow. Once he had swallowed, I pointed behind me. "Go give one of those guys a bite. Don't worry, we'll make sure Robert doesn't go anywhere."

Reyes walked past me and tentatively held the beef jerky toward the nearest ghoul. It slowly grasped the jerky, took a bite, and swallowed. Then, it hit the ground, just like the other two had.

"What?" Reyes whirled around wildly, like he thought someone might jump out of the bushes and tell him he'd been pranked.

"You didn't kill him," I said. "And Robert didn't kill those other two. Like Justine said, we will explain everything. We promise to answer all of your questions."

I heard a loud exhale, and I knew it was coming from Justine.

"Now we have three bodies to deal with here," Reyes said dully.

Justine slowly walked up to Reyes and took his hand. "I know it's confusing and scary. But when you examine these bodies, you'll find they weren't killed by anything they ate tonight. In fact, they were dead long before they showed up here. You'll find the real causes of death, and you'll likely discover at least some of them were murdered."

"Like the first victim found on the trails," I said. "The decaying body with old stab wounds, but a fairly fresh bite of steak in its mouth."

"How did you know about...?" Reyes shook his head. "I know, I know. You'll tell me later." He pulled his hand away from Justine's and ran it across his forehead. "I'm taking Mr. Pace to the station. Please, tell me all of you will be gone by the time I get back with a full team to sort out these bodies."

We all nodded.

Reyes looked at Justine. "I'll be at the Sanctuary first thing in the morning for all these answers you're promising me."

"Of course," Justine said, her voice barely above a whisper.

As soon as Reyes turned to lead Robert in the direction of the trail, Clara dashed up to Justine and pulled her into a tight hug. "It'll be okay," Clara said soothingly. "He'll understand."

"I sure hope so," Justine said, then sniffed.

"Well done, Olivia," Malcolm said. He lifted his top hat and nodded once.

"Now," Damien said, looking at the cave entrance, "it's time to find out if my father is inside."

CHAPTER TWENTY-SIX

Damien squared his shoulders and began to walk toward the cave entrance and the two ghouls still guarding it, but Malcolm called, "Wait!"

When Damien turned, Malcolm said, "There could be dangerous things inside. We shouldn't all go in, and anyone who does go needs to be prepared for anything."

Damien immediately looked at me. "I'm sorry, Olivia, but he's right. You should stay out here."

"But," I began, then I stopped myself. "As much as I want to go with you, I'll probably be of better help out here. I'll work on conjuring safety for those of you who go in."

"And we will stay with Olivia," said Morgan.

"To work a counter spell for any curses on that cave," Madge added.

Maida didn't say anything, but she took my hand and led me a short distance away, where we could all work on our magic without being in arm's reach of the ghouls.

Clara came to stand with us, too. "As curious as I am to know what's in there, it's smart for some of us to wait outside. If things go badly, the rest of us have to be ready."

Culver shrugged. "Guess I'm staying with all of you."

Damien, Malcolm, Fiona, Justine, and Zach approached the mouth of the cave, but the ghouls moved forward to intercept them. Fiona pulled something out of the pocket of her black pants and held it out to one. It was some kind of food, which the ghoul eagerly accepted. She then passed something to Malcolm, who made the same offering to the other ghoul.

Poor Reyes. He's going to be so dismayed to come back and find he's got five bodies to deal with instead of three.

With the ghouls out of commission, Damien and the others went inside the narrow mouth of the cave. I nervously tapped a hand against my thigh as I ticked off the seconds. I tried to push down my fear and focus on our safety and success.

We had only been standing there for a few minutes when a blast of cold air washed over me, and I sucked in my breath.

Maida giggled. "They're free!"

"There go the ghosts who were trapped," Morgan said.

I took that as a good sign. It made me feel more calm, and it encouraged me to keep conjuring. I didn't know if my work was making any difference, but it couldn't hurt.

A short while later, Justine emerged from the cave, her arm around a pale woman whose long auburn hair was hanging down in front of her face. The woman walked slowly, her feet tripping over the rough ground.

"Don't worry," Justine said. "Our vampires will help you."

Madge made a quiet noise of sympathy. "Gunnar is still patrolling overhead. We'll have him return to the Sanctuary to let Mori and Theo know they're needed."

Justine helped the woman lower herself onto a nearby rock as the three witches stood in a circle, chanted something quietly, then lifted their arms toward the sky. A teal beam of light shot up, and I had to avert my eyes because it was so bright.

The magical beacon lasted for only a second, but

Gunnar clearly knew what it meant, because he soon swooped down out of the sky and landed next to the witches.

Morgan pointed at the woman sitting on the rock. "This vampire is starving. Mori and Theo are needed."

Fiona came out of the cave just then, a black box clutched in her hands. "There are many dark-magic items inside," she said. "A ghoul was guarding this and other things. We'll have to safely dispose of them."

Make that six bodies for Reyes to deal with.

"Leave it to us," Madge said, taking the box carefully.

"So, you found the place," Gunnar said, a small smile on his face. "I look forward to hearing the full story." He extended his wings, and he kicked up a cloud of dirt as he launched into the air.

I watched as Fiona disappeared inside the cave again, and I was still gazing at the spot when something dark moved in the shadows. I felt a brief flare of fear before I realized it was Malcolm's coat swinging around his legs.

Damien was close behind Malcolm, and as they came into the clearing I saw they were holding a large gold birdcage between them. Behind the thin bars, I saw a beautiful red bird that nearly filled the entire cage. Even in the dim light from the stars overhead, I could see the way the feathers shimmered with orange and golden hues.

The bird had a sort of hunched look, like it wasn't sitting up straight on its perch. There were a couple of bald patches where its feathers were missing, and it seemed weak, or very old.

But what did I know? I had never seen a phoenix before.

"Damien, is this your dad?" I asked.

Damien looked at the phoenix, which turned and gazed at him serenely, its mottled beak making its profile look especially dramatic. "I think so."

Malcolm and Damien set the cage on the ground, and Damien opened the door. "Come on out. You're safe now."

But the phoenix sat motionless, continuing to stare at Damien.

"There are ashes in the bottom of the cage," Malcolm noted. "That supports our theory that Baxter was being forced to go through the life cycle of a phoenix in order to produce ashes. Bird, then flames, then egg, then bird again. How awful."

"All so the Night Runners could make some money on the supernatural black market," I said, horrified.

"That, and use the ashes and feathers for their own magical purposes," Damien reminded me. He turned to the witches. "Ladies, can you do a spell to make him human again?"

Morgan shook her head. "That is magic beyond our knowledge."

Madge nodded. "We will have to wait patiently for Baxter to do it himself."

Out of all of us, Maida was the only one who looked overjoyed to see the phoenix. She bounded up to the cage, bent down so she was at eye-level with the bird, and enthused, "Welcome back, Baxter!"

"If it is him," Damien said quietly. "My mother told Lucy that what we sought was hidden underneath. If she's known all along where my father was, why didn't she tell us sooner?"

I shook my head. "I'm not sure she did know. Even if she did, maybe she wasn't strong enough yet to communicate that information. Remember, Lucille seems to be waking up, in a sense."

In answer, Damien just sighed heavily.

"What are we supposed to do now?" I asked after a long silence. Before any of us had known Baxter was a phoenix, I had expected and hoped that, one day, we would find Damien's dad, and he'd come home to the Sanctuary. And I had naturally assumed Baxter would be human.

"We take him to the Sanctuary," Malcolm answered.

"No," Damien said. "I think he should go home. To the mine, I mean. We know it's warded, and there's only one entrance to the place. He'll probably be safer there. I'll be there with him, and when I'm at work…"

"When you're at work, we can all look after him at the Sanctuary," Malcom finished, his voice firm. "You're right that the mine is a secure location, but there's also a lot to be said for being surrounded by friends."

"Magical ones, at that," Clara said. She laughed, sounding both happy and relieved. "Look how gorgeous he is, even in this state. Once he's recovered from being imprisoned, he'll look spectacular."

"Magical friends or not," I said, "what if Sam Hart comes looking for him? Or even that guy Denny from the other faction?"

"I doubt we have to worry about that," Malcolm said. "We'll keep a watch for them, but it's likely they'll all be leaving Nightmare. By the end of the night, we'll have destroyed the dark magical items inside the cave, and people like Baxter and the vampire will be under our guard. There's nothing left for Sam, or Denny, or even Culver to stick around for."

I looked toward the spot Culver was standing, staring longingly at the entrance to the cave. "His plans sure backfired," I said, "but knowing he didn't kill Vincent makes me dislike him a little less. What do we do with him now?"

"Let him go," Damien said. "I'm guessing he's anxious to see Nightmare in his rearview mirror."

Damien and Malcolm wanted to get Baxter to the mine as quickly as possible, but Malcolm also wanted to stay behind to continue ridding the cave of anything dangerous. So, I volunteered to help get Baxter to Damien's car and then on to the mine.

We were still picking our way through the underbrush when I regretted the decision. Helping to carry a birdcage had sounded like no problem, but Baxter was a big bird, and he was heavy.

Luckily, help came in the form of Theo. He and Mori were running down the trail toward us, moving at their faster-than-human speed, when Damien and I finally stepped onto it.

"Mori, go find that vampire," Theo said. "I'll help Olivia."

Mori paused, just for a moment, her golden eyes fixed on the birdcage. "It's so good to see you, Baxter." She blew a kiss at the phoenix, then ran past us in the direction of the cave.

"Thanks, Theo," I said as he took over for me. Now that we were back on the trail and didn't have to watch out for plants trying to attack our ankles—and now that I was no longer lugging half the weight of a phoenix—we moved much more quickly.

When we reached the parking lot, Damien unlocked his car with his free hand, and I opened the passenger-side door. "Oh. Um, Damien, I don't think this is going to work," I said.

"He'll fit," Damien countered confidently. He and Theo tilted the cage and tried to slide it into the front seat of Damien's Corvette, but one side of the cage bumped up against the dashboard. "Maybe, if we lay the seat back, we can lay the cage down."

Watching my boyfriend and a vampire try to put a phoenix, who happened to be my boyfriend's dad, into the front seat of a sports car was just too much. I started gigging, and when Damien and Theo paused in their awkward maneuvering to look at me, I waved toward them. "Do you know how ridiculous this whole scenario is? Besides, the cage isn't going to fit. I appreciate your determination, but there's no way you're getting it inside the car."

"She's right," Theo said with a laugh. "It's so much easier if you take mine." He pulled a set of keys out of his pocket and handed them to Damien.

"I thought you and Mori got here so fast because of your super speed," I said. I was slightly disappointed they had arrived in such a normal, non-magical fashion.

"What can I say? We're lazy vampires."

Theo's car was a small SUV, and the birdcage slid right into the back of it. Theo wished us luck, then took off down the trail to go help the others.

Soon, it was just Damien and me. And the phoenix, of course.

Damien usually drove way too fast for my taste, but he took things slow as we headed for the old mine he called home. His eyes were on the rearview mirror nearly as much as they were on the road.

"He'll be okay," I assured Damien. "That cage isn't going anywhere."

"I know." Damien took a deep breath and let it out slowly as he braked for a stop sign. "I keep worrying I'll look in the mirror, and he'll have disappeared. It doesn't seem real that we have him back."

"It doesn't seem real to me that your dad is a bird."

As Damien pressed on the gas pedal again, he chuckled quietly. "Good point. For more than forty years, I had no idea my father was a phoenix. But look how quickly everyone who's seen him has said hello or welcomed him back. Our friends don't care what form he's in. They're just happy he's home."

"That's because we have great friends." I smiled,

thinking of the way Maida had greeted Baxter with so much joy. "And we'll all be keeping an eye on him. I'm still worried the Night Runners are going to want their treasure back."

"We'll worry about that if and when the time comes. For now, I just want to enjoy our victory tonight."

We drove in a happy silence the rest of the way to the mine. When we got there, we quickly moved the birdcage inside. As quickly as I could go while lugging that heavy thing, at any rate.

Once we were inside and the rusted iron door was closed and locked behind us, Damien looked at me with a grin. "You solved another murder. I'm so proud of you."

Damien leaned in to kiss me, but I pulled back. "Ew, not in front of your dad!"

"Later, then, when he's not looking. In the meantime, what do you suggest we do?"

"Now, we count the minutes until we can call Mama without waking her up." I looked at my watch, which told me it was already after two o'clock in the morning. "I can't wait to tell her that we found her brother-in-law."

CHAPTER TWENTY-SEVEN

Baxter sat and watched silently with yellow eyes that almost seemed to glow. His cage had been cleaned, but he himself still looked ragged. Some of his feathers had fallen out, and he moved slowly on his perch. His eyes, though, were quick and alert, and he seemed to be following the conversation happening around him.

"You're saying Aunt Lucille could talk to ghosts," Nick was saying. "Now, her ghost is talking to Lucy."

"Yes, exactly," Mama said.

Nick's eyes were the same brilliant blue as his mother's, and he shut them briefly. When he opened them again, he turned his head toward Lucy, who was sitting on the floor of the dining room, her arms wrapped around Felipe. "Lucy, honey, how do you feel about your great-aunt talking to you in your mind?"

Lucy looked up with a smile. "I thought it was neat the lady had the same name as me, but it's even better that she's family! I have a ghost in my family tree!" Lucy returned her attention to Felipe, who was beginning to chew on Lucy's curls.

"Lucy claims she saw my ghost once, when my heart briefly stopped after I was electrocuted." Mia, Lucy's mother, was gazing placidly at her daughter. "Plus, there have been other incidents that made me think she had a connection to the other side."

Nick's mouth fell open slightly. "This doesn't scare you?"

Mia shrugged. "My mom grew up in a haunted house. Ghosts don't scare me. Nor do those who communicate with them."

Nick shook his head incredulously. "Married for almost fifteen years, and I never knew you believe in ghosts." He looked thoughtful for a moment, then shrugged. "If Mia and Lucy aren't worried, then I guess I shouldn't be, either."

"Actually, I think a little worry is good. We want Lucy to pursue her abilities safely," Damien said. He and I had remained silent for most of the talk with Nick and Mia. It seemed better to let Mama handle telling them their daughter was a budding psychic medium who had begun communicating with Lucille.

Mama had insisted on bringing Lucy and her parents to the Sanctuary for the momentous conversation, while Benny had agreed to stay behind and mind the motel. She said part of it was her desire to see Baxter, and part of it was so he could "be included in the discussion," even though he couldn't actually speak.

Despite our late-night adventures at the state park, I had gotten up early that morning so I could be at the motel office the moment Mama arrived. I had originally planned to call her with the news that we had found Baxter, but it seemed better to do it in person.

It was a good thing I had made that decision, because she cried for five minutes straight, while I just hugged her and cried a bit, too.

"There's a psychic here at the Sanctuary," Mama continued. "Lucy has met her on her visits here, and she would be a good mentor for Lucy. I'll make sure you two get to meet Vivian, but I know you'll like her as much as I do."

Vivian, Amos, and the ghosts would be back by the next day. As soon as Malcolm had finished helping clear out the cave, he had called and told them to come home, since the search was over.

"We'll take all the help we can get," Mia said. "Nick and I are grateful Lucy has that kind of support." Mia leaned across the table and squeezed Mama's hand. "And we're grateful for you and your sister. I wish I could have met her."

"She was one of a kind. Still is." Mama stood up, grumbling about how benches were too complicated for old ladies, then pressed a hand against the birdcage. "See you later."

"Come on, Lucy, we're heading home," Nick called as he and Mia stood, too. "That's such a strange-looking dog."

Mama and I exchanged a glance. She and I, along with Damien, had agreed not to tell Nick and Mia everything just yet. They had *ooh*ed and *aah*ed over what a beautiful bird Baxter was, but we hadn't told them what kind of bird he was, or that they were related to him through marriage.

One supernatural secret at a time.

Lucy got up after saying goodbye to Felipe, then ran over to the birdcage. "Cheer up, pretty bird," she said. "You're family, too."

Lucy waved wildly at Damien and me, then followed her parents and Mama out the door.

"Did she just…?" I trailed off.

"She doesn't know it's Baxter, but she's clearly picking up on something." Damien put his arm around my shoulders and kissed the top of my head. "We did the right thing telling Nick and Mia how extraordinary their daughter is."

"Yeah." I wrapped my arms around Damien. I was exhausted but happy. The killer had been caught, Baxter had been recovered, and I was with people I loved.

The expression on Justine's face when she walked through the dining-room door half a minute later dampened my mood a bit.

"Well, I just had the talk with Luis." Justine plopped down on the bench across from Damien and me. Unlike our talk with Nick and Mia, Justine had decided to tell Reyes everything about the supernatural world.

"And?" I prompted.

Justine gave a resigned shrug. "And he didn't run away screaming. He actually said it explained a few things he'd never been able to make sense of."

Some of those things, undoubtedly, had been related to murder investigations. I expected Reyes might be talking to me soon, wanting to get a new look at a few of the cases I had gotten myself tangled up in.

"How does Officer Reyes feel knowing his girlfriend is supernatural?" Damien asked gently.

"I'm not his girlfriend. We've only been on a couple of dates."

Despite Justine's statement, I could see the little smile on her lips. She liked the idea of being Reyes's girlfriend.

"To answer your question, though," Justine continued, sitting up a little straighter and holding her head higher, "I think he might be even more interested in me now that he knows. He was pretty impressed when I slid a cup of coffee toward him telepathically."

"I'm sure Luis is using his newfound knowledge to get better details from Robert, too," I said.

"Luis said Robert was allowed to make a phone call, and it was to another hunter who promised to track down Sam Hart. As far as we know, Hart took off sometime while we were still clearing out the cave."

"Good," Damien said. "Hart needs to be brought to justice for making ghouls and trying to kill Olivia."

"He was really trying to kill Culver," I pointed out. "I was just collateral damage. But, yes, I'm glad to know Hart is unlikely to get away with his actions."

"And the police are giving the hunter information to help him find Hart," Justine continued. "The normal world and the supernatural world have collided when it comes to catching bad guys."

"It's wild how many people know about the supernatural now," I said. "First, we found out that Emmett has known for ages—"

"And even brought down a ghoul!" Damien noted.

"And now Rey—I mean, Luis—knows, and Lucy's parents are learning about psychics and ghosts."

Justine smiled. "Our family is growing."

As if in answer, the phoenix squawked loudly. It was the first sound Baxter had made since Malcolm and Damien had found him inside the cave.

All three of us turned to Baxter, only to see his body erupt into flames. It looked like a fireball was trapped inside the birdcage.

I gasped and began to stand, though I wasn't even sure what I could possibly do to help.

"It's okay, Olivia," Damien said, pulling me back down onto the bench. "He's a phoenix. This is what they do. After he burns, he'll be reborn from the ashes. He was looking so bad when we rescued him that I anticipated this."

I sighed with relief and relaxed as the heat from the phoenix warmed my cheeks. "And," I said, "while we wait for his transformation, we can all celebrate. Baxter is home."

A NOTE FROM THE AUTHOR

Reader, when I started this series, I had no idea what direction things would go with Damien's missing father. I knew what kind of supernatural creature he was pretty early on, but I didn't know where he was or how Olivia and her friends would rescue him. I never expected Lucille to start showing up to help out, either.

One of the things that makes this series such a joy to write is how often I'm surprised at the unexpected things that happen. I often don't feel like I'm making up the story. Rather, the story is already there, and I'm as excited as you to know what happens next.

I hope you feel the same sense of fun and excitement with this series. Before you head over to book 10, will you please leave a review for *Terminated at the Trailhead*? It helps other readers find my work, and I appreciate your help.

Eternally Yours,

Beth

P.S. You can keep up with my latest book news, get fun freebies, and more by signing up for my newsletter at BethDolgner.com!

Body at the Bakery

NIGHTMARE, ARIZONA BOOK TEN
PARANORMAL COZY MYSTERIES

Rolls, Real Estate, and Reunions in Nightmare, Arizona

When a despised landlord is found dead inside Nightmare's popular bakery, Mama Dalton worries one of her friends is the prime suspect. She takes a cue from Olivia Kendrick's amateur-sleuth success to dive into the case, bringing Olivia along with her into a world of old grudges, soured relationships, and secret back-alley meetings.

At the same time, an arsonist is at work in Nightmare, threatening the historic buildings that make the former Wild West town iconic. Olivia, Mama, and the supernatural staff at Nightmare Sanctuary Haunted House must team up to keep Nightmare safe by tracking down the guilty party.

While trying to solve the murder and stop an arsonist, Olivia is also busy helping Damien Shackleford piece together the mystery of his long-lost mother. His father would probably help, but Baxter is in no state to talk. Damien's family is heading toward an unconventional reunion, whether he's ready for it or not...

ACKNOWLEDGMENTS

As always, it takes a village to produce a book. My beta readers—Kristine, Sabrina, Alex, David, Lisa, and Mom— help me polish the story. Lia at Your Best Book Editor and Trish at Blossoming Pages are my intrepid editors. Jena at BookMojo puts the whole package together with her beautiful cover design and formatting. My ARC readers are a mighty team who help with early reviews. I am so grateful for everyone who helps me get from an outline scrawled in a notebook to a published book!

ABOUT THE AUTHOR

Beth Dolgner writes paranormal fiction and nonfiction. Her interest in things that go bump in the night really took off on a trip to Savannah, Georgia, so it's fitting that her first series—Betty Boo, Ghost Hunter—takes place in that spooky city. Beth also writes paranormal nonfiction, including her first book, *Georgia Spirits and Specters*, which is a collection of Georgia ghost stories.

Beth and her husband, Ed, live in Tucson, Arizona. They're close enough to Tombstone that Beth can easily visit its Wild West street and watch staged shootouts, all in the name of research for the Nightmare, Arizona series.

Beth also enjoys giving presentations on Victorian death and mourning traditions as well as Victorian Spiritualism. She has been a volunteer at an historic cemetery, a ghost tour guide, and a paranormal investigator.

Keep up with Beth and sign up for her newsletter at BethDolgner.com.

BOOKS BY BETH DOLGNER

The Nightmare, Arizona Series

Paranormal Cozy Mystery

Homicide at the Haunted House

Drowning at the Diner

Slaying at the Saloon

Murder at the Motel

Poisoning at the Party

Headless at Halloween (Novella)

Clawing at the Corral

Axing at the Antique Store

Fatality at the Festival

Terminated at the Trailhead

Body at the Bakery

The Eternal Rest Bed and Breakfast Series

Paranormal Cozy Mystery

Sweet Dreams

Late Checkout

Picture Perfect

Destination Wedding (Novella)

Scenic Views

Breakfast Included

Groups Welcome

Quiet Nights

Halloween Vibes (Novella)

The Betty Boo, Ghost Hunter Series

Romantic Urban Fantasy

Ghost of a Threat

Ghost of a Whisper

Ghost of a Memory

Ghost of a Hope

Manifest

Young Adult Steampunk

A Talent for Death

Young Adult Urban Fantasy

Nonfiction

Georgia Spirits and Specters

Everyday Voodoo

Made in the USA
Monee, IL
01 March 2025

13203217R00125